M000203695

THE SPLINTERED CROWN

A TANKARDS AND HEROES NOVEL

LARRY N. MARTIN

SOL

eBook ISBN: 978-1-939704-88-7
Print ISBN: 978-1-939704-89-4
The Splintered Crown Copyright © 2019 by Larry N. Martin.

The right of the author to be identified as the author of this work has been asserted in accordance with the Copyright, Designs and Patents Act 1988.

No part of this book may be reproduced in any form or by any electronic or mechanical means, including information storage and retrieval systems, without written permission from the author, except for the use of brief quotations in a book review.

This is a work of fiction. Any resemblance to actual persons (living or dead), locales, and incidents are either coincidental or used fictitiously. Any trademarks used belong to their owners. No infringement is intended.

Cover art by Joachim Kornfeld, cover wrap by Melissa Gilbert
SOL Publishing is an imprint of DreamSpinner Communications, LLC

CONTENTS

THE SPLINTERED CROWN

A TANKARDS AND HEROES NOVEL

By Larry N. Martin

TOM AT THE POXY DRAGON

"GOT ANY ALE THAT DOESN'T TASTE LIKE DONKEY PISS?"

The stranger's companion laughed heartily at his friend's joke and didn't seem to notice that the regulars at the bar took a step away from them. The bard in the back stopped his song mid-stanza.

"Don't know what you're complaining about," Tom, the bartender, replied. "That's a step up. Used to taste like donkey's balls. And before that—"

"Gods and cuttlefish, man! How about your whiskey then? I just want something that doesn't taste as bad going down as it might coming back up, if you know what I mean," the stranger said.

He looked like the sort of man who would find his way to the Poxy Dragon tavern—big, tall, inked, and mean as a wolverine. His shoulder-length dark hair was greasy and tangled, and his long beard had braids and brass beads in it, like that made him a pirate. Tattoos in black and red wound around both arms and peeked from the throat of his tunic. One, a black snake, slithered its way up his bicep. Tom figured that was as good a name as any for the stranger, Snake. Not like it mattered. He wouldn't be back.

Snake's buddy stood half a head shorter and maybe twenty pounds lighter, *probably his lookout and lackey*, Tom thought. No tattoos. Reddish blond hair and a beard to match, he looked at least a decade younger than Snake. "Red" would do.

"Suit yourself." Tom poured a glass of the house whiskey and slid it to Snake. He kept his expression unreadable, although if Snake and Red knew what was good for them, they'd have taken note of the way the regulars leaned in to watch but didn't get any closer.

Snake tossed off the shot and thumped his chest like he'd proven something. Red hooted, as if taking the drink was an accomplishment. Tom and the others waited for the reaction.

Three...two...one....

"What...what..." Snake tried to say something else, but between the way he gasped for air, lips working like a fish out of water, and the tears running down his face from the potent liquor, he was in too much distress.

"What did you give him?" Red demanded. "You poisoned him!" His face grew as red as his hair, and he looked as if he intended to go over the bar at Tom.

Tom wasn't worried. Red probably weighed less than the sack of cabbages in the kitchen.

"Should I dig a hole out back?" Thaddeus had wandered in at the first sounds of distress. The old undertaker had his favorite shovel, Bessie, slung over one shoulder. Mud caked his pants and dirt streaked his face and hands. Tufts of white hair stuck out over his nearly bald head and peeked from inside his ears. He looked at Tom with great excitement, anticipating the task.

"Probably not," Tom replied, as Red pounded on Snake's back and Snake gripped his throat with both hands as if that would reduce the feeling of scorched flesh in his mouth. "I imagine he'll come around."

"I'll hang out for a bit, in case he doesn't," Thaddeus said with a sage nod. "He's awfully fat. 'Twould take me a bit longer than usual to dig a hole that big." He gave Red a look up and down. "I can throw the skinny one in on top, for free."

"I'm not dying!" Red yelped. He tugged on Snake's arm, trying to get him to leave, but he might as well have tried to move a tree. Snake stayed bent over, wheezing and alternating between braying like a donkey and honking like a duck. His face had gone crimson, sweat dripped from his brow, and the veins in his neck stood out.

"Did you bewitch him? Is that what you've done?" Red drew a knife from his belt.

"You don't need that pig-sticker, son." Gunnar, one of the tavern regulars, looked up for the first time since the altercation started. "I'd put that away before someone gets hurt."

Red's eyes widened, as Snake gave a particularly loud bleat and fell to his knees with a crash. "*Before* someone gets hurt? What do you call *that*?"

Gunnar raised a shaggy eyebrow. He'd been a mercenary, long ago. Now he looked more like a great brown bear, big, solid, and hairy. Snake might be rippling muscles and bravado, but Tom knew that, even now, Gunnar could clean the tavern floor with the newcomer, although he probably couldn't be arsed about it.

"I'd say the man just lost his cherry to Tom's whiskey. Happens to everyone. You never forget your first time. Damn near choked on my tongue, I did," Gunnar recalled with pride, and tossed off a double shot of the same whiskey without apparent effect.

"Bloody bognuts!" Red looked at the men at the bar as if they had all escaped the asylum. "If your whiskey's this bad, I'm glad we didn't eat the food!"

Chairs scraped on the floor as the men at the bar left their seats and drew back toward the fireplace on the other side of the room, except Gunnar. Tom leaned on his forearms at the bar, like he was about to watch a show. Even the patrons sitting at tables took note, moving farther into the common room or turning their chairs for a better view.

All but a one-eyed blond who sat alone near a boarded up window, smoking an intricately carved pipe. She favored Red with a tepid smile, but Tom bet that when the newcomer met the gaze of her good eye, he'd feel ice slither down his back.

"Who said it?" a harsh voice sounded from one side of the bar. "Who insulted my food?" A thin woman with gray hair and wizened features strode from the kitchen, brandishing an iron pan like a cudgel. She rounded on the nearest man, who was twice her size. He shrank back at her fearsome gaze.

"Was it you?" Elsie demanded, raising the pan for a punishing blow. A lifetime of hefting sacks of flour and wrestling hog carcasses onto a spit made her lean and surly. In the back of the tavern, the men near the fireplaces whispered among themselves and money changed hands, as Constance the tavern wench collected their bets. Tom wondered if Red knew the odds were not in his favor.

"That madman at the bar poisoned my friend!" Red argued, tugging more desperately at Snake's beefy arm as he stood. Snake's eyes weren't quite as bugged out as they'd been before, nor his lips as swollen, although the beet red color of his face made Tom fear the man might have a weak heart.

For a moment, the heavy pan remained suspended over Red's skull, and Elsie's stare bore into the man, deciding his fate. Then the pan came down with a swish as Red cringed, but it never touched him. Elsie twirled it in her bony hands, showing off the ropy muscles in her arms. "Ah, well then. You can say what you like about the whiskey— it's total shite."

She moved so fast Red yelped when he found the skillet suddenly shoved under his chin. "Just don't be talking about the food, you understand?"

Tom thought he caught a whiff of piss and saw a dark stain on Red's pants. Thaddeus had been on his toes, eager for a new project, but he rocked back with a glum look of disappointment. In the back, the bettors muttered as Constance distributed their winnings, then made another round of collections on the next wager, since Red and Snake had yet to leave the Poxy Dragon.

"You're all mad!" Red huffed. He watched, alert as a cat in the dog catcher's pen, as Elsie retreated into the kitchen, and jumped when Gunnar slapped the bar for another round. Tom obliged, and Gunnar didn't flinch as he drank it down in one go, then belched and thumped his broad chest with his fist.

The regulars came back to their seats at the bar, and Lucas, the kitchen boy, came around to gather up the empty plates and tankards.

"Look, mate, are you going to order, or not?" Tom asked. "You're causing a ruckus."

"You nearly killed him!" Red shot back, pointing at Snake. The big man's breathing rasped like a consumptive, and his shirt was wet with sweat despite the cool evening.

Tom raised an eyebrow. "Looks all right to me. Hey Thad, you think he's a goner?"

The undertaker gave a mournful shake of his head, clutching his shovel with both hands. "Afraid not."

"You're all fawkin' lunatics!" Red said. "You're dangerous, that's what you are. I'll report you to the sheriff!" He froze when he felt cold steel against his back.

"Nobody goes to the law, no one gets hurt." With his gangly frame, hands and feet too large for the rest of him like a big puppy, Lucas's voice was deeper than most people would expect, given that he was barely seventeen. He held the tip of the knife against Red's skin without flinching.

"I like my job here, and these are my friends," Lucas said evenly. In the back, Constance took a new round of bets. Gunnar turned to watch. The regulars gestured for another round, and Tom waved them off, watching the show.

Hope came into Thaddeus's eyes once more. The one-eyed blond looked amused.

"I was j-just kidding," Red lied, and this time when he heaved with his full weight against Snake, the big man budged, just a bit. "I swear, we don't want more trouble."

Lucas's big brown eyes and young face might make a foolish man underestimate him. Given how Red had paled, he might not be quite the fool Tom took him for. Red's gaze flickered to where Constance gathered wagers.

"Hey. Don't look at her," Lucas warned, poking Red with the knife. "She's not for you. You aren't good enough to lick the horse shit from her shoes."

"What do you want?" Red's voice came out as a reedy whine. "I've got a bit of silver. You can have it. Just don't kill us."

"How about you and your friend move on, and have a care how you pick the next place you stop for a drink?" Lucas withdrew the knife and stepped back.

"Sure. We're l-l-leaving," Red stammered. "Come on," he urged his buddy, tugging with all his might. He dug his heels in on the sticky wooden floor and barely made Snake shift his weight.

"Let me help." Tom came around from the bar. There was no hiding his limp, but just because the injury had sidelined him from his old life, it didn't stop him from taking out the trash.

Red's eyes grew wide when he got a look at the hole in Tom's leg, impossible to hide even with pants. "What...what happened to you?"

"Wyvern," Tom snapped, eyes darkening. In the back, money changed hands again when Red blurted the question-that-should-not-be-asked. "Don't like to talk about it. Thanks much for bringing it up." His deep voice sounded like ground glass, and he towered over Red and even had an inch or two on Snake, who looked up, eyes red from tears and straining for breath.

Gunnar sighed and slid off his bar stool, barely fazed by the whiskey. He shouldered Red aside, then gave him a shove toward the door. Tom got under Snake's left arm, while Gunnar grabbed his right bicep, and together they hoisted the big man off his feet as if he weighed nothing. Red scrambled out of their way, practically falling over himself to get to the door first and open it for them.

"Tell your friends not to come," Tom said as he and Gunnar heaved Snake out into the night.

"Right. Yes. Got it," Red promised, in such a hurry that he jumped the three steps down to the ground.

Tom shook his head, and closed the door, then dusted off his hands. Gunnar took his seat at the bar and slid his glass across for another round.

The regulars settled up with Constance, who sashayed her way up to the front, looking pleased with herself. Pretty as she was, none of the tavern's regulars let their gaze linger or their hands roam. Not after what happened to Stumpy.

Benny, the bard took up where he'd left off, singing a tragic tale of heroes and failed quests. A few of the patrons threw coins in his direction, but whether that was in payment or to make him stop, Tom was never quite sure.

"Made more off the bets than you did from the liquor," Constance said, handing over a bag of coins to Tom. "And after all that, they even managed to leave before things got really exciting."

Excitement wasn't hard to come by in Kortufan. As a crossroads for trade, a hive of villainy, and a proving ground for thieves, the town had plenty of travelers to fleece, deals to go badly, and fortunes to be lost. Spies, assassins, and mercenaries, arms dealers, smugglers, and informants dealt in the town's most valuable currency—information.

Lots of taverns in Kortufan were home to dealmakers and brigands, but only the Poxy Dragon was a proving ground for heroes.

Outside in the town square, the bells tolled eleven. Tom's head came up, and his attention went to Lady Leota at her table by the shuttered window.

"It's time," the seer said. Lady Leota had chosen the Poxy Dragon as her own, no matter how many times Tom tried to urge her to reconsider. He'd given up long ago and learned to live with his tavern being the parlor for a demigoddess.

Some said that Leota was the bastard daughter of Harran, the god of war, and Revienne, goddess of fate and memory, inheriting some of her father's power and all of her mother's opinions. Tom had a sneaking suspicion the rumors were not only right but probably left out the most important details. He'd decided that he couldn't fight Fate.

Lady Leota stepped back. Everyone in the tavern turned their attention to the wall beside her. The old window began to glow, first like the rays of dawn struggled from behind it, and then as if the fires of the Inferno burned within. Men threw their arms up to shield their eyes, but no one moved. The tavern's regulars knew what to expect and counted the show to be worth the price of the awful ale.

A vortex opened within the bright light, full of swirling colors and starlit black streaks as if someone had stirred a sunset and the night sky in a witch's cauldron. Tom caught a whiff of sulfur and the scent of dead fish and brackish water. A panicked seagull erupted from the vortex, squawking and flapping, so befuddled that it flew right into a solid wall. Elsie picked up the stunned bird without comment and trudged back toward the kitchen.

Next, a tall human in blood-spattered leather armor staggered through the portal. He stood as tall as Tom, broad-shouldered and solidly muscled, with short-cropped dark hair and cold gray eyes. An array of weapons hung from his belt. He carried a body across one shoulder, that of another fighter whose ashen skin and stillness told a tale of loss.

The portal flared again and out stumbled a dwarven woman, war axe in hand, face inked with the battle runes of her people. Tom noted the black dot by her right eye, a mark of mourning for a fallen comrade. Behind her came a female warrior, whose inky skin and curved ears marked her as a dark elf. Her slight build masked her strength, because she was supporting the last member of the expedition with one arm, bearing his full weight. At least the blond fighter was still breathing, although he pressed one hand against a seeping wound on his side.

The tall human approached Lady Leota with a murderous look in his eyes. She did not flinch, her expression unreadable.

"We got what you sent us for," he spat. "Can't say it was worth the cost." He dug out a stained velvet pouch from beneath his cuirass and dropped it into her hand.

"You have done a great service," Leota said in a cool voice that carried in its inflection an echo of millennia.

"Can you heal Jof?" the warrior demanded, with a jerk of his head toward the corpse he carried on his shoulder.

Leota's face reflected sadness and acceptance. "I cannot."

"Then how about Dev?" the warrior begged, glancing to the wounded man who barely remained on his feet.

Lady Leota nodded. She stood and stepped toward the injured man, and nudged his bloodstained hand aside, replacing it with her own. She raised her face toward the ceiling, closed her eye, and murmured something the others couldn't hear. Sparks like foxfire danced around where she touched him, green glimmers of light. After just a few heartbeats, the injured man's color improved, and the blood flow stanched. Moments later, he straightened and carefully examined the unmarked spot on his belly that was all that remained of his wound.

"Thank you, m'lady," he said, falling to his knees in front of Leota. The hint of a smile touched her lips, and she bid him rise.

"You are my heroes, and you have done well. Your quest will save the lives of thousands, and help bring peace to that land. You have proven yourselves, your deeds will be remembered, and your names will be celebrated in the halls of the gods."

Tom moved toward the tall human, who looked a bit poleaxed. "Welcome back," he said. Thaddeus joined him, eyeing the dead man as if he were mentally calculating the size of the grave to be dug. "We'll see that your friend has a proper burial in the cemetery out back and that you and your team have food, drink, and a room to rest."

"When you're rested, I'd like to hear your tale, for the ballad I'll write about you," Benny the bard piped up. "I've got the tune and a few verses already, but it's the details that keep people singing your praises long after you're gone."

Gunnar came over to carry the body, and the fighter drew back, still protecting his charge. "We'll do right by him, I swear," Gunnar said quietly. "There ain't a more honored burying place for heroes in all of Kortufan or the kingdom of Trinadon than Warrior's Rest in the field behind us."

Reluctantly, the tall human allowed Gunnar to take the body of his fallen comrade. "You'll do him proper? He died bravely."

Gunnar gave a solemn nod. "We will. Light a pyre for him as well, if you want to come and spill some liquor in remembrance." He cradled the body in his arms, then turned and followed Thaddeus out of the tavern as all of the patrons stood and bowed their heads.

Lucas led the bloodied heroes up the back stairs to their room. Tom knew that Elsie had expected at least some of them to return, so she'd have their dinner ready shortly. Constance circulated among the patrons, who paid up on their wagers on the returning party of adventurers.

Benny tuned his lute, then launched into his new song, immortalizing this latest group of heroes. In his younger days, Benny caught the attention of all of the ladies of the court and no small number of the men, who swooned over his beauty and his voice, praising his skill with his instrument and his gifted tongue. A few twists of fate brought him to the Poxy Dragon, where he now served Lady Leota as the tavern's permanent bard-in-residence.

Tom brought a goblet of absinthe to Lady Leota and watched the emerald liquor sparkled in the candlelight. She accepted it with a nod of thanks. Up close, Tom thought he could see the strain in her beautiful features, and wondered if even a demigoddess grew weary of loss.

"It can't always be helped." Tom figured he was a fool, trying to comfort an immortal, but it seemed like the right thing to do. Gods, it happened so often. Sometimes, none of the party returned, and the quest would be assigned to a new group of would-be heroes. Others returned maimed in mind or body. The price of fame was dear, though the number of applicants never waned.

"No, but that doesn't make it any easier," Lady Leota said, sipping the absinthe. "For all my abilities, I can't see their future when they come to me. And if I could, I don't know that would matter."

Probably not, Tom thought. Far too many people would rather be dead and famous than alive and forgotten. He'd had his turn at glory, and nearly lost a leg and his sanity to it. He pitied the fighters who applied for their chance to make a name for themselves, but he didn't envy them.

"I'll be all right," Leota assured him. They weren't exactly friends—a mortal and an immortal really couldn't be—but there was fondness between them. "I always am," she added, looking away. Tom guessed the truth of it; that as with any commander the knowledge of the cost weighed heavy on the seer's mind.

"See to your guests," Lady Leota said, taking her seat. "There'll be a new group of heroes tomorrow."

2

KIERON

"As if this job could get worse," Kieron Lucero muttered under his breath. His companion, Mitchell Calderon, grimaced in agreement.

"You there! Guards! Get into place and watch the cargo. I'm not paying you to gossip." Alphonse, the overfed merchant who had hired them for this job, glared at them. "There are brigands in these woods. I need you to stay sharp!"

Kieron and Mitchell had worked lousy jobs before. Kieron's military background, along with his impressive height and strong muscles, made him a natural sell-sword – despite having the face of an angel, curly brown hair, and blue eyes that won over the ladies.

Mitchell's past was more brawler than soldier, but even those who didn't guess that he was a wolf-shifter knew to keep their distance. They took one look at his muscular build, slate gray hair, and yellow eyes, and knew a predator when they saw it.

Jobs had been scarce, and money tight. Normally, Kieron and Mitchell could pick and choose. But lately, with the bad harvest and some unrest to the north, caravans and traveling merchants weren't plentiful. He'd been too quick to agree to the job and let down the people depending on his judgment. There would be time to berate himself for his mistake later. They'd signed on without asking enough questions, and this is what it got them. Trouble.

Alphonse reminded Kieron of a slug, all the more so once he and Mitchell discovered what the cargo actually was.

People. They'd been hired by a fawking slaver.

Kieron's molars ground together. As soon as he and Mitchell had found out, they'd made plans. But as Kieron knew well from his time in the army, things could—and did—go wrong, even with the best strategy. And what the two of them had dreamed up didn't come close to being anyone's "best" plan. On the other hand, it beat the shite out of the alternatives.

Aside from Kieron and Mitchell, their party included Alphonse, the wagon driver, two other guards who had probably been hired out of an alley behind a local tavern, and the hapless prisoners in the wagon. Alphonse, Kieron, and Mitchell rode their own mounts. The other guards either rode with the driver of the wagon or walked beside it.

Kieron had stolen a look inside and counted five men and women, likely bought from the debtor's prison in Kortufan. The wagon that carried them was a big wooden box with a single, barred window. A heavy lock secured the door. Kieron had listened for the drag and clink of manacles, relieved when he only heard the shuffle of feet and low voices.

The Rhone Forest cut a swath across the kingdom of Trinadon, impossible for travelers to avoid. The steep Shahoran Mountains and the white-capped rapids of the mighty Tellgran River restricted the paths of the highways that cut through the forest. Regular caravans and honest merchants took the Royal Road, which had its muddiest areas planked and benefitted from regular patrols of His Majesty's soldiers.

Alphonse was anything but honest, so their assemblage of hard-worn wagons made its way along the lesser routes, where mud up to the axels sucked at the wheels, and it was anyone's bet whether fallen trees might block the road or a recent storm had washed out part of the road. On the back routes, the only advantage was a lack of soldiers who might take an interest in illegal cargo.

Kieron didn't have a problem escorting honorably ill-gotten gains.

"Honorable" as in stolen from people who wouldn't miss them. But he hated slavers. So as soon as he and Mitchell realized what they'd landed themselves in, they'd made arrangements.

He glanced at the forest on both sides of the road. Tall trees lifted a canopy high overhead, making for sparse underbrush. Even so, trailing vines, rotting trees, and uneven terrain made for dangerous footing, so most people kept to the road. Only a madman would ride cross-country—

Howls and shouts echoed in the stillness, followed by the thunder of horses' hooves. Three riders closed in, two from one side and one from the other. They were clad in black, and kerchiefs covered their faces. Their horses vaulted fallen trees and leaped over gullies, as the brigands cut the wagon's group off before and behind.

"Do something!" Alphonse bleated. He pulled a sword from the scabbard at his belt, but obviously had little real experience in a fight from the way it wobbled in his hands.

Kieron and Mitchell traded glances, then rode up behind the two erstwhile guards, thwacking them soundly in the head with their staves. Alphonse's two hired ruffians dropped to the ground.

"Help!" Alphonse yelled, as one of the brigands rode up to him, sword in hand, and disarmed the slaver with ease.

"Get off your horse," the rider ordered. "On the ground. Hands were I can see them." Alphonse complied, but his jowls quivered with fear.

"Take my money! Just take it and be gone!"

"Don't want your blood money," the brigand replied. "I want to see your kind rot in the Pit. Now get on your belly and put your hands behind your back."

"Oh gods, oh gods. I'm going to die," Alphonse squeaked.

"You might wish you were dead when the king's men get through with you," the brigand muttered, hog-tying the slaver out of sheer pique.

"I'm just the driver!" The wagon master shrieked. "Don't kill me!"

One of the newcomers looked to Kieron for guidance. Kieron shook his head. He'd seen enough to know that the wagon driver knew what cargo he carried and didn't care. The second brigand grabbed the driver's arm and pulled him out of his seat, making short work of tying him up.

The third brigand slipped around to the back of the wagon and had the lock open in less than a minute. Kieron swung the doors open, and the prisoners blinked at the sudden light.

"Come on, come on. We don't have all day. This is a rescue! Now, move your arses!" Kieron growled.

The prisoners scrambled out, and Kieron was glad to see they looked to be in good enough shape to walk back to the main road. The freed slaves glanced around, unsure.

"Go on, get out of here," Kieron urged. "You're free. The road's that way," he added with a jerk of his thumb. "Don't go back to Kortufan. Now hurry!"

Needing no further urging, the prisoners fled.

"I'll see you hang!" Alphonse threatened, glowering at Kieron and Mitchell.

Kieron gave him an unpleasant smile. "Slavery's illegal in Trinadon. The way I see it, we just did the king's guards a favor." He bent down and picked up the cloth purse Alphonse had offered as ransom, and counted out enough coins for the pay promised to Mitchell and him, dropping the rest beside the slaver. "Honest pay for honest work."

"We need to get going." One of the brigands looked to Kieron. "There are more riders heading this way, not far down the road."

Kieron trusted the mage's foresight. "You heard him! Ride!" He and Mitchell followed the others back through the forest, leaving Alphonse and his unlucky partners behind.

The ride through the forest was wild and mad, and Kieron loved every minute. His blood was high from the fight, although truth be told Alphonse's party had offered pathetically little resistance. Kieron's lip curled as he thought about the big man who had no qualms about enslaving unfortunates but begged like a coward for his own life.

They rode hard until they were almost back to the main road. The lead "brigand" slowed in a clearing, waiting for the others to catch up. The three newcomers tucked their kerchiefs back into the neckline of their shirts, revealing their faces.

"You know he'll come after us," Kane Hodge said, tucking a strand of red hair behind the delicate point of one ear. Her features and her talent as a thief favored her human mother, but her skill on a horse and with a bow came from the elven heritage of her father.

"Figured as much. We needed to find a better place to stay anyhow," Kieron replied.

"There are only so many hovels we can afford," Mitchell pointed out. "Not counting the ones we've been thrown out of."

"I can shield us long enough to grab our things, and then lay a distraction spell to make it hard to track us," Declan Willard offered. Crow black hair hung lank in his eyes, only partially covering the scar that cut through one eyebrow and down his cheek. His striking blue eyes would have been memorable without Declan's height, which put him a few inches taller than Kieron and a head above many men. Those features also made it harder for him to hide.

"If that fat bastard comes after us, I'll make sure he gets a proper welcome," Malyn Sana promised. "The ghosts at the rooming house don't like his kind. They'll give him a fright and then some." If anyone had a harder time than Declan when it came to fitting in, it was Malyn. Slender and dancer-graceful, the healer-medium's white-blond hair and fine features were striking, even without the kohl that rimmed his bright blue eyes or the aristocratic manners that were the last vestige of the privilege Malyn had left behind.

"At least I took our pay," Kieron said. "It's enough to keep a roof over our head and food on the table for a few days, at least."

"That's more than we've often had," Mitchell agreed. "Speaking of which, I'm hungry. Let's go."

All the way back to Kortufan, Kieron berated himself for getting them into a bad situation. *If I'd paid more attention, asked more questions, we wouldn't have ended up like this. Malyn and the others could have been hurt, or caught by the guards. Alphonse is going to send his men after us, and even in the back alleys of the Dregs, there are only so many places to hide.*

"It's not the first time we've had a job go belly up," Kane said, riding up alongside him. "Quit beating yourself up over it."

"I should have known better."

Kane cocked an eyebrow at him. Her good looks got her past many a guard, who later came to regret it when they found their masters' valuables missing. If those guards had paid more heed to the intelligence and calculation in her eyes, they might not have been such easy marks. She was Kieron's oldest friend since he'd come to Kortufan, dearer than a sister, someone he trusted with his life.

"Last time I checked, Malyn was the seer, not you," she replied. "And we didn't end up running off with no coin to show for it."

"We'll have to move."

Kane shrugged. "I won't miss the rats. They're bigger near the slaughterhouse. Maybe we can find a place that's suitably haunted and that doesn't smell of blood."

Malyn always preferred to rent rooms that were haunted because they were often cheaper, and he enlisted the ghosts as lookouts and watchdogs. The others had made an uneasy peace with their spectral roommates. Kieron rarely minded, except for when the ghosts made their already-chilly rooms even colder, or brushed against him, sending a shiver down his spine. Mitchell was the only one who grumbled about the spirits, saying that they raised his hackles, something his inner wolf couldn't completely ignore.

The five of them made an unlikely team. Yet somehow, despite their differences in background and opinions, it worked, most of the time. Kieron met Mitchell in jail when Mitchell was injured from a fight and unable to completely control his shifting. Kieron recognized a fellow fighter down on his luck and had taken him in when they finished their sentence.

Kane found them. She'd turned up on their doorstep with an offer of even shares of the heist she was planning if they'd be the muscle to help carry the loot.

Months later, Malyn approached the three of them at a local tavern, sashaying up like he owned the place. He had claimed to have had a vision that promised them gold and glory if they formed a team, along with a mysterious fifth man. A few months later, Malyn's foresight and a helpful ghost led him to Declan, a mage whose power—and perhaps, his mind—had been shattered in a fight with another sorcerer. Malyn had been adamant about taking Declan in and nursing him back to health. Declan had come a long way since then, though dark dreams still troubled him, and he might never be completely whole. Still, the five of them were stronger together than they had been on their own, proving Malyn's visions right, yet again.

Kieron led them back to Kortufan by a different route than the one used when they'd left. It would take Alphonse time to get word to his henchmen in the city, and by then—with luck—Kieron and the others would have disappeared into the slums of the kingdom's biggest trading hub. Plenty of people lost themselves in Kortufan; the trick was being able to do it when someone was in pursuit.

They found a stable for their horses and Kieron paid the groomsman enough to assure their mounts would be fed and cared for, with an extra coin to win the man's silence and good graces. It was a little farther away from their rooms, but they couldn't risk using the same place they had before. The stable owner glanced warily at their party. Mitchell gave people pause, even when he was in a good mood. Kieron figured it was unlikely that the stable master would want to be on Mitchell's bad side, so their horses were safe.

They'd headed toward their lodging house by a meandering path that cost them time but made it less likely that anyone followed them. Though Kieron couldn't shake the sense that someone was watching. Between Kane's thievery and the minor larcenies they committed to keep body and soul together, they'd made plenty of enemies. So while Alphonse might not have had time to sic his goons on them yet, he'd have to stand in line for a chance at revenge.

They reached the rooming house where they had been staying, a ramshackle three-floor building awkwardly squashed between two larger and more solidly-built neighbors. The foundation must have shifted, because the house had a definite slant. From the narrow alley across the street, stray cats yowled, more interested in courting or fighting than in chasing the rats, or maybe scared off by their unusual size. There had been nights when work had been scarce enough to make Kieron consider trapping one of the large rodents. He shuddered. *Thank the gods and demigods, they hadn't sunk that low—yet.*

"I've got a hunch about a place that might have room for us," Mitchell said as they neared their lodging house. "Far enough away that we won't be easy to find."

"Go check it out. I'll pack your things," Kieron promised. "The sooner we're out of sight, the safer we'll be." Mitchell nodded, then turned off at the next side street, with a promise to meet them at the fountain in the square on the other side of the neighborhood.

Declan cast a distraction spell to make passers-by pay less attention. The magic wouldn't make them invisible to anyone who was specifically looking for them, but it would make onlookers less likely to notice or remember them.

It didn't take Kieron long to pack. He threw his threadbare extra clothing into a bag, along with his bedroll, blanket, and a tarp for camping. Then he did the same for Mitchell's things. He heard the sound of tin clanking as Malyn grabbed their few pans and the pot they used for coffee. There wasn't much food to pack—some dried fruit, cheese, and smoked sausages, as well as a hunk of bread—but they weren't in a position to waste. Within minutes, the four of them had gathered their belongings as well as stripping the two rooms of all their shared possessions, down to the firewood.

Kane went downstairs to stand watch, and Declan bounded up, grabbing his amulets and the supplies he used for magic—a chalice, some odd ingredients and potions, and a few items Kieron figured were best not examined closely. In less than half a candlemark, they were done, and the room was bare.

Helga, their ghostly roommate, watched their activity from the corner, arms crossed, clearly disapproving. She was strong enough that all of them were able to see her translucent form, but only Malyn could hear her.

"Why's Helga angry?" Declan asked Malyn. "I thought she didn't like our card games."

The seer shrugged. "She liked us better than the old man who lived here before. She says he didn't bathe, and he farted too much."

"Good to know she has standards," Kieron commented. "Maybe the next tenant will be a trollop with a slew of clients. That should make for more interesting evenings."

"I've asked her to cause problems for anyone who comes looking for us." Malyn walked over to the corner, where Helga's ghost stood, and made a little bow. "Thank you, kind lady, for watching over our fire at night, and frightening off the people who came to rob us. We are grateful." He pulled a wildflower from his vest that he had plucked on the ride back, and laid it on the floor.

"Even the dead swoon for him," Kane remarked, rolling her eyes.

Malyn gave a sly smile. "I'm just good at making friends."

"Go on down," Declan said. "I'm going to cleanse the room so that if someone sends a mage after us, he can't pick up traces of our energy."

Kieron and the others trooped downstairs, carrying everything they owned. If any of the rooming house's other boarders were curious, they knew better than to pry. In this part of town, a web of streets appropriately called the "Dregs," minding one's own business led to a longer life. The tenements slouched on either side of the narrow alleys, blocking out the sunlight. Lines heavy with washing hung overhead, strung over the road between the buildings. Cooking smells from places all over the kingdom mingled with the odor of horses, garbage, and chamber pots. Kieron didn't much mind leaving, but he had no illusions that their next place would be better.

They split up into pairs, taking separate routes to the meeting point, just in case. Kieron walked with Malyn, while Declan and Kane headed off in a different direction. Four people carrying bulging packs might be remembered. Declan's magic couldn't wipe the memory of onlookers, it just made the recollections a bit fuzzy, unimportant. Still, better not to tempt fate more than they usually did.

Malyn had the distracted expression he wore when he was talking with ghosts. Kieron had been surprisingly distressed to realize just how many restless spirits haunted the ginnels of Kortufan. Then again, people landed in the Dregs because they had nowhere else to go, so maybe their ghosts felt the same. Kieron really hoped his future held better, but Malyn stubbornly refused to cast lots for any of their groups, saying that they would make their own way.

"Anything?" Kieron asked. He made sure Malyn didn't step off the curb, and nudged him away from the worst of the refuse piled along the gutter. In a half-arsed attempt at stealth, Malyn had tied up his white-blond hair in a scarf. While that hid his unusual hair, it just drew attention to his fine features, beautiful for either a man or a woman, and difficult on first glance to discern which he was. Malyn was happy to play up that confusion, claiming that being neither and both came with his particular psychic abilities.

"The guards came through earlier, looking for pickpockets," Malyn murmured, passing along the information he learned from his ghostly informants. "The woman who lives on the second floor of the building on the right poisoned her lover when she found out he cheated on her. The old man in the first floor rooms of the gray building will likely die by morning."

"How do you stand it?" Kieron asked. "The living talk too much as it is, and you hear the dead as well!"

Malyn shrugged. "It's always been this way, so I don't know any different. My family thought I was lying when I told them. Or maybe, in hindsight, they did believe and were afraid of what I'd find out. Anyhow, that's why I'm here instead of there." His tone was deliberately indifferent, but Kieron doubted that the split had been painless.

"More to the point, is anyone looking for us?" Kieron kept his eyes open and his wits sharp. Pickpockets and cutpurses were the least of their worries. Individually and together, they'd come to the attention of the constable for petty theft, and under suspicion for larger infractions. Few people could utilize the dead as lookouts, but coins spread around in exchange for gossip could net the guards dangerous information. Kieron had no desire to reprise his stay in jail.

"Not for all of us, no," Malyn replied, averting his gaze.

Kieron looked at him. "Explain. We agreed that an enemy for one is an enemy to all."

Malyn sighed. "There's a witch-hunter in town and a wolf-finder. Don't know if they're working together. I barely evaded the witch-hunter two days ago, and I hoped he had left town, but there's no way to know. I didn't want to alarm Declan, because he worries too much as it is. I'd actually planned to take care of the son of a bitch myself."

"You know Mitchell and I will help. Kane too."

"Mitchell's got his own problem with the wolf-finder. If the jailers knew he was a shifter, then he's been registered, and all the wolf-finder has to do is figure out where to hunt him."

"Over my dead body," Kieron said, feeling his anger rise. "When were you planning to tell the rest of us? Or was Mitchell just going to run off in the night?"

Malyn grimaced. "I doubt Mitchell intended to run. We're his pack now."

"And he'd sacrifice himself to save us."

"I wasn't trying to keep secrets from Declan," Malyn went on, worry creasing his beautiful features. "It's just...you know how he is. He'll make himself sick over it, living out a hundred ways it could all go wrong. And he's only just coming back to himself."

Kieron had come to value Malyn's insights. As a healer as well as a psychic medium, saying that Malyn had a unique perspective was an understatement. Despite his penchant for showmanship, Malyn hid a practical outlook and strategic mind behind the kohl and silks he used as camouflage.

"So perhaps moving isn't a bad thing after all," Kieron replied. "Better than being ambushed."

"We've all made enemies," Malyn replied. "It's just a question of whose enemies are after us at any given time."

"This witch-hunter, is he nearby?"

Malyn cocked his head, listening to a voice only he could hear, and Kieron assumed that meant communing with ghosts. "Not at the moment. I've recruited the ghosts who are willing to be my lookouts, but they can't be everywhere, and they aren't always aware."

"What can Kane and I do to help?" Kieron had pissed off plenty of people over the course of his twenty-eight years, some badly enough for them to want revenge. Vengeance and blood money were the underpinnings of Kortufan's daily commerce. Business deals, love affairs, even something as petty as which street vendor to buy lunch from got tangled in the complex web of favors and paybacks.

He'd navigated that dangerous dance alone, and ended up in jail, only a few steps from the noose. But in the year since the five of them had formed their tattered little adoptive outcast family, they'd not only managed to stay out of the dungeon, they'd also had food in their bellies and kept a roof over their heads. Kieron would be damned if he'd let a couple of bounty hunters destroy what they had built.

"I don't think those hunters are looking for us, specifically," Malyn replied. "We haven't done anything to attract attention lately. Shifters are always in season. And there's a standing bounty on 'practitioners of dark arts and necromancy,' which means anything the tribunal wants it to mean."

His gaze roamed, fixing on spots where Kieron could not see anything and guessed he was watching the ghosts whose spirits never departed these wretched alleys. Kieron kept an eye out for living threats. It was a toss-up, in his opinion, which were more dangerous.

Kieron felt suddenly exposed and vulnerable, and his right hand went to the pommel of his sword. He held his breath, waiting for something to go wrong as they neared the meeting place. To his relief, he found the others waiting there, equally jumpy.

"Where's Mitchell?" Kane asked, glancing around the square. Kieron did not overlook the dagger she'd palmed, ready to strike if need be.

"I'm right here, and I found a place." Mitchell stepped out of the shadow of a large temple. Kieron noticed that his friend had a sheen of sweat on his forehead despite the cool weather, and seemed a bit twitchy, like he'd run into trouble. Mitchell caught Kieron looking at him, and gave a slight shake of his head. *Not now.*

"Let's get out of the open," Kane suggested. "We've used up our good luck for the day."

Mitchell led them down a twisting path of narrow alleys and passageways between buildings, but Kieron realized that the convoluted route offered many different options, and he smiled to himself at the wolf's cleverness. Wolf or man, Mitchell thought like a predator, and he could flip that logic to reason out the best escape when they were the prey.

"Here," Mitchell said, stopping in front of a narrow building that rose three floors high, with a steeply gabled roof and a half-timbered stucco construction on the upper stories. Smoke and dirt had turned the white stucco a dingy gray, and the door was in dire need of a coat of paint. Right in the middle of the door, someone had scrawled a quarantine symbol.

"You want us to go in here?" Kane asked, regarding Mitchell as if he'd lost his mind. "Do you mean for us to catch our death?"

Malyn's gaze lost focus for a second, then he looked up. "It's gone. Whatever sickened the people who were here before, the malady is gone."

Mitchell looked smug at the vindication. "I've already been inside. There's nothing left from the old tenants, and sage smudging and a few open windows will put it right."

He led them inside, and Declan called a flame of cold hand fire to light their way. Kieron closed the door behind them to shut out prying eyes but stayed near one grimy window so he could watch for an ambush.

"Besides, I doubt you and I could catch anything, even if the ill humors remained," Mitchell said to Kane. "Wolves and Elves don't usually sicken from human illness. Malyn's healer magic keeps him well, and I figured Declan could do a protection spell to cover him and Kieron."

His yellow eyes gleamed in the dim light. "Don't you see? It's the perfect cover. We leave the mark on the door, and common thieves won't want to enter. If you climb to the roof, there's a narrow gap between this and the next buildings on either side, so we can run the ridges if we need to. Go out the back, and there's a five-way split in the road a block away. Plus there's a basement that leads into the old cellars. I didn't have time to check, and I blocked the door so no one can come in that way, but that's a bonus." He grinned. "And best of all, no other lodgers, and no landlord."

Mitchell looked extremely pleased with himself, and Kieron wondered if his friend had been scouting for new lodgings for them before Alphonse made a move necessary. He wouldn't doubt it. Mitchell thought like a general, always gaming the situation out and running through scenarios in his head, looking for options. Kieron admired that ability. He tended to run with the best option at the moment and make it up as he went.

While Mitchell spoke excitedly about the new lodgings, Declan walked purposefully, left to right around the empty room. He paused at the fireplace and laid a hand on the bricks, then nodded to himself and continued his circuit. The house was three rooms deep, with a central stairway.

Malyn wandered over to the steps and peered into the darkness. Kieron heard him speaking softly but couldn't make out the words.

"It'll do," Declan announced when he rejoined them. "Whatever caused the sickness wasn't a curse. There's no trace of magic here, good or ill. I can ward it for us without a problem."

"There are two ghosts, both upstairs," Malyn reported. "They are agreeable to us moving in, and willing to help." He nodded. "I think it'll work."

Kieron and Kane exchanged a glance. "Well?" he asked the half-elf.

Kane shrugged. "No side windows make it easier to defend, and I like the roof access. From what I saw outside, the upper windows would work well to shoot from, if it came to that." Kane was the undisputed master archer of the group. "It's bigger than we need, but we don't have to actually live in all of it."

Kieron had thought the same. "All right. Good hunting, Mitchell. Let's get settled in."

It didn't take long for them to unpack their meager belongings and stake out places to sleep. By unspoken agreement, they spread out only on the first floor, finding the three adjacent rooms to be far more space than they'd had before, and not wanting to be out of sight of each other.

Kieron used the wood they'd brought with them to start a fire, while Declan wove his wardings and Malyn sat on the steps, getting to know the ghostly residents better. Kane climbed to the second and third floors to have a look around, sizing up the angles from the windows to the street for defense.

Mitchell went to fetch water from the fountain in a nearby square and returned with a few more logs, a full wineskin, and a loaf of bread from a street vendor. "We won't starve," he announced, laying out his treasures.

Kane put a pot of tea on the fire. The others spread their cloaks on the floor in front of the fireplace, and Kieron figured they were all feeling the effects of a long, eventful day. He set out the sausage, cheese, and other provisions they'd brought with them for a cold supper. The food wasn't fancy, but there was enough for a decent meal.

Kieron stretched out, feet toward the warmth of the hearth, and watched the flames. "I just want one big score," he said, daydreaming aloud. "Make enough to quit this wretched city and move to the countryside. Buy land to raise sheep and chickens, and have a vegetable patch. Brew some beer. Wouldn't have to steal or fight anymore—and there'd be room for all of us to do as we please, without the constables looking down on us."

Kane's expression was difficult to read. "Really? All of us, on a farm?"

Kieron heard the skepticism in her voice but refused to take it to heart. "Sure. Why not? Elves don't much like cities, so you tell us. All. The. Time. Fewer ghosts to jangle Malyn's nerves, plenty of room for Mitchell to roam in his fur, and we could grow the plants Declan wants for his potions. No more running from the guards, or getting shot at, or going hungry."

"Sounds good to me," Mitchell said. "Nothing like taking my wolf on a night run without having the dog catcher after me."

"The city's as crowded with ghosts as it is with people," Malyn said, taking a swig from the wineskin. "Not that there aren't ghosts in the countryside, but they're not all mashed on top each other. I like the plan."

"Could I have a room, just for books?" Declan asked. "I can't keep many here because we move so much, and they're heavy. But I need them for my magic."

Kieron smiled. "You can have all the books you want."

Kane cut a piece of sausage and a slice of cheese with her knife. "Well, I guess I could make do," she allowed, a smile playing at her lips. "Seeing as how the rest of you think it's a good idea."

"Now all we need is the money," Kieron said with a sigh. "But it's nice to think about, anyhow." Making that dream come true might be next to impossible, but at least for tonight, Kieron resolved not to give up hope.

3

MITCHELL

IF HE'D BEEN BORN A DOG SHIFTER INSTEAD OF A WOLF, THINGS MIGHT BE SO much easier, Mitchell thought. Not that he wasn't proud of his wolf—thick, silver pelt, black markings, fierce teeth. He'd seen his reflection in still water and thought he made a handsome animal. When they rode through the countryside and he could get away with it, Mitchell loved to cut loose and run. Yes, he scouted for danger, but mostly it was the sheer joy of the freedom his wolf afforded that drove him.

Those chances were few lately. To get out of the cursed city with its smoke, stink, crowds, and noise, they had to line up a job. Something to guard or something to steal. And with the problems to the north and bad weather, the caravans that usually provided both options were fewer than usual.

He and Kieron had gone out to look for work, something that would involve all of them, preferably. Kieron headed for the pubs, where traders and patrons often went to find willing workers for a job, legal or not. Mitchell set out for the docks, where he could at least feel the wind in his hair if he couldn't run free through the forest.

One of the most traveled crossroads in all of Trinadon sat just outside Kortufan. The harbor on the other side of the city opened onto the Blue Gulf, where the Deniter River flowed into the Broad Sea.

Ships from across the kingdom and beyond came to trade in Kortufan, provisioning the caravans that took their wares inland to the manors and towns, and also to the palace itself.

But the winter had been harsher than usual, with rough seas that wrecked ships and floods that damaged the bridges caravans needed to reach the interior. Fewer ships meant less cargo, and not as many merchants, cutting down on how many guards were needed. Mitchell worried where the next job would come from. They had some coin put by—another benefit of pooling their resources. But even being frugal, their money wouldn't last long.

"You know anyone looking for caravan guards?" Mitchell asked Hamden, one of the dockworkers who usually knew everything about the shipments just arrived and due into port.

"Wish I did," Hamden replied, pausing and wiping the sweat from his brow. His dark skin glistened despite the cold breeze off the ocean, and his voice held the lilting accent of the southern kingdoms beyond Trinadon's borders. Hamden had come to Kortufan aboard one of those cargo ships and never left. "Most of this is going to the warehouses, for now."

"If you hear of anything—"

Hamden shrugged. "Check back with me tomorrow. Things change. Good luck."

Mitchell crammed his hands into his pockets and made his way down the waterfront, checking at every ship being unloaded, and then working his way back, stopping at each warehouse. Merchants and shipowners who had hired Mitchell and his friends in the past just shook their heads.

Kieron's fantasy of living on a country farm where they wouldn't go hungry and had plenty of wood to stay warm grew more appealing as Mitchell came away from his inquiries without a solid lead. He knew Kane intended to make the rounds of her less reputable contacts, to see if someone needed anything stolen. Thieving wasn't Mitchell's first choice, but he didn't care for hunger or cold, and running off to hunt rabbits proved much more difficult in the city.

He hunched his shoulders against the icy wind coming from the ocean. In his wolf form, the cold didn't bother him, but as a human, he minded the winter, all the more when his belly was empty. Mitchell glanced around the wide open space between the first street of warehouses and the wharves. He couldn't shake the feeling that someone was watching him, but when he glanced around—carefully, so as not to call attention to himself—he didn't see any likely suspects.

The smell of meat pies and fried fish from the street vendors made him even hungrier, but he didn't have coin to spare. Surely some caravans and merchants were trading, even if at only a fraction of their usual volume. He resolved to try one more street of warehouses, and then set off for the stables to see if any of the wagoners for the traders, peddlers, or caravans might be in need of hired help. That kind of work was a notch or two below the sort of jobs he and his friends favored, but it was mostly honest work, compared to thieving, and it didn't risk the constable coming after them.

The docks smelled of fish and salt breeze, mingling with the scent of spiced, cooked meats and the odor of horses. Mitchell wrinkled his nose when he passed sailors who had obviously gone too long aboard ship without a bath, or the wind shifted and he caught a whiff of kelp. Even in his human form, Mitchell had an exceptional sense of smell. On days like this, he considered it to be a curse.

The third street of warehouses had much less traffic. The buildings looked older and shabbier, since the more prosperous merchants preferred locations with easier access to the wharves. Shadows stretched across the narrow alley where taller buildings blocked the sun. Mitchell shivered, remembering the tales he'd heard that parts of the waterfront had been built over old cemeteries from the city's original settlers.

Something about the alley gave him pause. Mitchell stood half a head taller than most men, solid with broad shoulders and a muscular build. Wolf or human, he didn't start fights but was happy to end them if trouble came looking for him. Still, he wasn't a fool. The dockside attracted rough characters. He scanned the street for loitering men or lurking vagrants and saw only a few wagon drivers and laborers. Just in case, Mitchell palmed a dagger from his belt, keeping it handy just in case. There was something...

A knife whirled through the air and sank deep into Mitchell's left shoulder. He cried out in pain, knowing almost immediately from the burn that the blade was silver, a poison to shifters. He pulled the knife from his shoulder and threw it down.

Two men emerged from the back door of one of the second street warehouses. Mitchell glanced behind him and saw a third man blocking the way he had come. The wagon drivers and laborers had vanished, unwilling to get involved.

Mitchell knew he had found the wolf-finders.

"Don't make this harder than it needs to be." The leader, a tall man wielding a wicked knife with a silver-edged blade, gave him a cold smile. "Your kind doesn't belong in the city, among decent folk."

"You include yourself in that?" Mitchell spat. "Because there's nothing decent about hunting down a man in cold blood." Already he could feel the silver like a spreading sickness, a flush of fever and a tightening in his belly.

"Good thing you're not really a man," the wolf-finder replied.

The poison in his system slowed his shift, but Mitchell still forced his transition before the others closed in, betting on his instincts and reflexes to save him. He'd long since learned to endure the blinding pain that came with his bones breaking and reforming as his body blurred and rebuilt itself in seconds.

Mitchell shook off his now-useless clothing and lunged at the leader, teeth bared, then sank his fangs into the man's right forearm, biting down with all his strength. The man shrieked and tried to kick him loose. Another knife whizzed by, barely missing his ear. Mitchell leaped at the second man, knocking him out of the way as he struck the hunter in the chest with his full weight. The man fell and Mitchell kicked off, digging in deep with his hind claws as he ran.

He never intended to fight. Mitchell just wanted to make an opening so he could escape. On foot, the hunters wouldn't be able to catch him in his wolf form. Then another silver throwing knife lodged in his hip, and Mitchell staggered. He'd already lost blood from the shoulder wound, which would have slowed him some, but he resolved to push through the pain for the distance it would take to lose his pursuers. But the knife in his hip made the leg give out, and he felt the additional silver like fire in his blood.

"Kill him slowly," the leader ordered, catching up. One of his henchmen picked up the long knife Mitchell's bite had forced him to drop. Blood dripped from the leader's mangled forearm, and Mitchell felt cold satisfaction that he had at least gone down fighting. The second hunter advanced, knife raised, and Mitchell prepared to die.

A woman's shriek pierced the gloom, echoing in the narrow alley. The temperature plunged, turning cold enough that Mitchell's breath misted and frost appeared where the rain gutters ran out into the street. The shadows grew darker and more ominous, and shapes moved at the edges of his vision.

The henchman paused. "What was that?"

"Who cares? Do it!" the leader urged.

A cold mist formed in the air, spreading and growing more dense as it filled the alley. One by one, ghosts took form in the swirling fog.

"Do you see?" the third man yelped. Mitchell began to drag himself away, hoping that he could put some distance between himself and his attackers, although he knew they would only have to follow the blood trail to find him.

The ghosts looked almost solid, their features as clear as their ragged shrouds. They howled and keened, coming at the hunters with arms outstretched and hands grasping, closing in until the hunters were forced to give ground. Their anger raised Mitchell's hackles and frightened his wolf. He wondered if he could see the revenants because he was dying from blood loss and the poison of the silver. But it was clear his attackers saw and feared the spirits as well.

One of them cursed and took off running. The leader glanced between the ghosts and Mitchell, unwilling to abandon his trophy. Mitchell knew that the bounty on shifters paid well enough to be worth the risk. The second henchman pulled at the leader's uninjured arm.

"We've got to get out of here, Liam!"

The leader shook him off. "Not without the wolf." He approached Mitchell again, shoving the second man forward to finish the kill.

Mitchell mustered all his remaining strength to snarl and snap. That made the henchman draw back, caught between the fearsome spirits and a wolf with nothing to lose. Liam pushed the man toward Mitchell, and he stumbled, nearly gutting himself with his own knife.

The spirits swept forward, even more of them now, clearly angered with the wolf-hunters. The second man shrieked and ran, leaving Liam injured and alone. He took one last look at Mitchell and must have guessed attacking with the knife in his left hand would be too great a disadvantage, even against an injured wolf. With a curse, he fled, and the ghosts chased him all the way to the end of the alley.

Mitchell collapsed onto the paving stones.

No one ventured out of the warehouses; maybe they had run off as well.

The poison made it difficult to breathe, and Mitchell's heart beat sluggishly. He'd escaped the wolf-finders with the aid of the ghosts, only to die in a gutter. He wouldn't make it back to the others, to his friends, his pack. That thought bothered him more than he expected.

A cloaked figure strode down the alley with a swagger that dared anyone to get in its way. The cape's swirl and its peaked hood made it difficult to judge size, and the face was lost in the shadow of the cowl. Mitchell braced for a new assault, perhaps even worse than the wolf-finders and then the scent hit him and his wolf let out a low whine.

The figure stopped beside him and dropped to his knees. "Come on, we can't stay here," Malyn said. He pulled the second knife from Mitchell's hip and laid a hand over both wounds. Mitchell felt the heat of Malyn's healing magic strengthening him, knitting together torn flesh.

"I can't get rid of the poison quickly," Malyn said. "But that should be enough for you to shift. I can't carry your heavy arse!"

Mitchell nodded and gave a weak yip in response before sniffing Malyn to take in the smell of pack. He mustered his strength and willed himself to change, as Malyn went to grab the clothing he had discarded. The ghosts remained around them, assuring no one would be foolish enough to interfere. It took more effort than usual to shift, thanks to the silver, and he couldn't hold back the whimpers of pain. The effort left Mitchell weak and sweating—and naked in the middle of the alley.

"Gods, I don't think I'll ever get used to seeing that." Malyn grimaced and shook his head. "Put these on," Malyn tossed him his pants, holding his coat and shirt. Between the two of them, they got him dressed and found his boots.

"Let's go," Malyn got under his uninjured right arm, and did his best to take some of Mitchell's weight off his bad hip.

"The ghosts—" Mitchell panted.

"Will stay in the alley a while to make sure no one follows." They hobbled as fast as Mitchell could force himself to go, grateful for Malyn's help. Although Malyn stood several inches shorter and had a much thinner build, he was stronger than he looked, all lean muscle.

"How did you find me?"

"I had a vision. Almost didn't get here in time. Took me a while to figure out where you were. Visions don't come with a map," Malyn huffed.

Malyn didn't have the kind of magic Declan could use to deflect interest or make them forgettable. Instead, he used what he could do— he spoke with ghosts to help them avoid constables and cutpurses on the slow, painful trek back to their lodging. More than once a ghostly warning had them dodging into a doorway or an abandoned basement to avoid dangerous interest.

All the while, Mitchell could feel Malyn's healing power seeping through, shoring up his scant reserves, and keeping him on his feet. He didn't know how much the drain was costing Malyn, but he resolved to find a way to repay him for the rescue.

"Accept the gift," Malyn murmured as they neared their quarters.

"What?" Mitchell wondered if Malyn could read his mind.

"I can feel you holding back. Don't. I'm a healer. I heal people. Someday, you'll save my arse. It's what pack does."

Pack. Mitchell strained to trust, even now, but he liked the sound of that. His wolf had already decided, but for the man letting down his guard was harder. It had been so long, after having been cast out of his own pack, left to fend for himself. For years he had believed he could do without, manage on his own. That had gotten him locked in jail where he nearly died of fever. Kieron had refused to abandon him, even at his surliest. Since then, their little found family had proven its worth over and over. Perhaps no one else would understand his mismatched pack, his family of choice, but Mitchell would defend them with his life.

"We're here. Let's get you off that bad leg."

Declan met them at the door, and Mitchell caught the bitter odor of one of the mage's potions. No doubt Malyn had told Declan to expect one or both of them would come back injured.

"You found him?" Declan crowded close, and Malyn shouldered past him to get Mitchell to the spot on the floor he'd claimed for his bed.

"Of course." Malyn sounded like there had really been no question. He eased Mitchell to the floor, and Mitchell felt relieved to lie down. The poison in his blood made his head spin and he felt like he was burning up.

"He's been cut with silver," Malyn said. "Do you have the elixir?"

Declan went to the table they'd scavenged from upstairs, and returned with a dented tin cup. "This should help," he said, tipping the contents slowly into Mitchell's mouth as Malyn supported him to sit. The concoction tasted like pond scum and smelled worse, but Mitchell believed in his friend's magic.

"Kieron and Kane?" Malyn asked as he settled Mitchell onto his back.

"Not back yet. Will he be ready to go, if they find us a job?"

"I'll be ready," Mitchell promised, although his voice sounded weaker than usual. "Don't count me out yet."

Malyn rolled his eyes. "The big bad wolf has spoken," he said, his voice dripping with sarcasm. He rattled off several ingredients and supplies, and Declan turned to fetch them.

"I'm not done with the wounds yet," Malyn told Mitchell, pulling back his shirt to expose the pink line that marked the first injury. "You're lucky that knife didn't hit sinew. I patched you up enough to get you out of that gods-forsaken alley, but both blades went deep, even without the poison of the silver."

Mitchell surrendered, lying still as Malyn worked on his injuries. He breathed as deeply as he could, letting the scent of his mates calm his wolf. Declan's potion quelled his roiling gut, which kept him from heaving up what little remained in his stomach. Malyn's touch was soothing, and Mitchell suspected the healer also drew out as much of the poison as he could.

When the gashes were closed, Declan brought a green, foul-smelling poultice, which Malyn slathered over Mitchell's injured shoulder and hip. He couldn't help wrinkling his nose or the scowl he gave Malyn.

"Yeah, I know. Smells awful, but leave it on until it turns gray," Malyn ordered. "It will draw out the remaining poison."

Malyn looked much paler than usual, almost translucent. Mitchell thought that the light must be playing tricks. The healer slumped, exhausted, and Mitchell guessed that lugging him back from the alley and then healing his wounds had badly taxed the man.

"You'll feel better in a bit," Malyn promised. "Maybe not up to catching rabbits, but better than you do now."

"Thank you." Mitchell's voice sounded more like a bark than his usual timbre. Despite the healing and potions, he still felt like shite. But the poultice warmed him, tempering the fever and chills from the poison, and he figured that if it made him sweat, that would help purge the silver as well. He watched his mates, worried that Malyn might have done too much.

Malyn managed a tired smile, and he made a dismissive gesture. "It would have been too quiet around here without you, and I'm rather fond of rabbit stew." He rose and stretched, then stumbled. Declan caught him and kept an arm around Malyn's shoulder—despite the healer's protests—to help him over to his bed.

"I'll wake you if there's a turn for the worse," Declan vowed. He had a tin cup with a different mixture for Malyn, who wrinkled up his nose at the smell, but gulped the elixir down without protest. "It's taken a lot out of you. Rest. I'll keep watch."

"Don't get distracted," Malyn grumped, already sounding sleepy.

Declan chuckled. "I promise I'll smite anyone who dares bother us. Is that sufficient?"

"That'll do." Malyn pulled a blanket over himself and fell silent. Declan moved a chair near the grimy window and sat where he could watch the street.

"Get some sleep, Mitchell. You look like shite," Declan said without glancing in the shifter's direction.

"I feel like shite, too." Though Mitchell no longer thought he was dying, which was a definite improvement. Deciding that he was as safe as they ever got, he closed his eyes and let himself drift off.

WHEN MITCHELL WOKE, night had fallen. Declan had stoked the fire, which warmed the room and gave off enough light to see. The sound of the door opening roused him as Kieron entered. One glance at the fighter's dejected face told Mitchell his efforts to find them a job had not been successful.

"Nothing," Kieron stormed. "How can it be that there are no caravans or supply wagons hiring guards?"

"Hush," Declan admonished, too late. Malyn groaned and rolled over, as Mitchell struggled to sit up.

"What's that smell?" Kieron asked, turning to notice Mitchell and Malyn. Mitchell glanced down at the poultice, which had turned dark gray.

"Medicine," Declan replied. "Mitchell was attacked. Malyn saved him."

"By who? The guards?" Kieron had gone from discouraged to furious in the space of a heartbeat.

"Wolf-hunter, I suspect," Kane said, descending the stairs. Mitchell guessed she had come across the rooftops, either to outrun pursuers or for the sport of it. "I heard there was one sniffing around. Figured I'd warn everyone when I got back. Looks like I'm late."

"Is he going to be all right?" Kieron looked closer at Mitchell.

"He just needs to rest," Malyn muttered.

"And what about you? You look like death warmed over. You did too much, didn't you?" Kieron accused.

"I'll be fine, just let me be for a bit." Malyn glared before closing his eyes.

Mitchell could see Kane watching them from where she sat on the bottom step. "And before you ask, I had a few nibbles for heists, but nothing I'd say was worth the risk. I'd rather pick pockets than work for a couple of those men."

"Nothing much from the harbor," Mitchell said, hating how weak his voice sounded. "I meant to check at the wagon stables, but I didn't make it that far."

"The flooding won't last, and the king's guards will get the unrest settled," Declan said. "Caravans will start back up again. It's always slow this time of year."

"Not this slow," Kane grumbled.

"I have an idea." They all turned to look at Kieron, even Malyn, who had rolled onto his side. "I heard about a pub called the Poxy Dragon, a day's ride from the city. They say there's a seer who sends out questing parties to make their name and earn their fortune. If they succeed, there's a bag of gold in it for them."

"There's got to be a catch," Kane said.

"Who pays the gold?" Malyn wondered aloud, his voice weak.

"It's probably dangerous," Declan chimed in.

Kieron looked to Mitchell. "Well?"

"If we can keep body and soul together until I'm back in fighting shape, I'm in. Not like we've got better things to do," Mitchell said.

Kieron grinned. "We'll be the best heroes the Poxy Dragon has ever seen."

4

TOM – TWO WEEKS LATER

No evening at the Poxy Dragon seemed complete without at least one bar fight. Perhaps patrons came eager to see would-be heroes get sent off on often-deadly adventures, but they would settle for common fisticuffs if no heroes happened to wander in.

Tom leaned against the backbar, gauging when, or if, to intervene. He'd had his share of getting clipped in the jaw and punched in the gut trying to break up fights, and he usually let the idiots batter themselves unconscious before he and Gunnar heaved their sorry arses out into the street. Of course, if someone was stupid enough to pull a knife or injure an onlooker, that changed things.

"You cheated!" The accuser was short but muscular, red in the face either from anger or too much of Tom's potent whiskey.

"Bollocks! You're the cheat, you son of a buzzard!" The other man stood a foot taller, broad in the shoulders and broader of belly, equally florid with indignation.

In the back, Constance moved among the regulars, taking bets.

Shorty threw the first punch, clipping Buzzard on the jaw. Tom gave him credit for brass balls because Buzzard probably outweighed him by fifty pounds. Buzzard barely seemed to register the punch, swinging a massive fist in return. Shorty bobbed and wove like a boxer, easily dodging, and landing a rabbit punch to the kidneys that had the big man staggering.

Some of the men in the back called Constance over to up their wagers.

"I want my money back!" Shorty demanded, ducking Buzzard's swing. Both men had drunk several rounds of whiskey, but Tom decided maybe he'd lost count of how much Buzzard had, because the big man should have been able to hold his own.

"You're the one who cheated me!" Buzzard roared. He ran at Shorty, arms outstretched to grab.

Shorty dropped to a crouch and put his shoulder into the big man's belly, flipping Buzzard over his back.

The crowd hooted, and Constance made another pass to collect money as wagers rose. Elsie came out of the kitchen, wiping her hands on her bloodstained apron.

"What's all the racket? I can't hear myself think in the kitchen with all this noise!" she admonished.

Buzzard hit the sticky floorboards with a grunt. Tom expected Shorty to throw himself on top of the big man and start swinging, but instead Shorty stepped away. "Look, all I want is my money back."

Buzzard came off the floor in a blood rage, roaring in anger. He pulled a shiv from his boot, and patrons who hadn't scattered drew back out of self-preservation. Gunnar slipped off his stool and cracked his knuckles ominously. Neither Shorty nor Buzzard were smart enough to take the hint.

Gunnar closed on Buzzard, but Elsie got there first. She swung a barstool at Buzzard's head, clipping him hard enough to break one of the wooden legs. The big man went down in a heap. Gunnar changed direction and grabbed Shorty from behind before he could make an unfortunate life decision, crossing his arms over the other man's chest and lifting him a few inches off the floor.

"For gods' sake, do I have to do everything around here?" Elsie asked, and turned to give everyone in the tavern her best stink eye. She dropped the broken barstool, dusted her hands together, and huffed.

"I came out here to complain about the sausage," she informed Tom. "The next time you buy on the cheap, make sure they grind up the rats' tails better. Found a whole one. That's way too chewy. I may do miracles, but I have my limits."

Several patrons at the tables pushed their plates away, gaining a greenish cast to their complexions. One man ran for the exit, hurtling over Buzzard's prone form. His loud retching triggered a small stampede. Tom groaned and wished again that Elsie would mind her tongue. She did perform miracles in the kitchen and could make almost anything taste good. Patrons loved her food – as long as they didn't know what was in it.

Tom glared at Shorty like it was his fault. "Get out, and don't come back for at least a week." Shorty bolted as soon as Gunnar dropped his hold.

Gunnar watched as Shorty barreled out the door. An exchange of curses suggested that Shorty had collided with one of the puking patrons. Gunnar gave a put-upon sigh and grabbed Buzzard by one ankle, lugging him toward the door and rolling him down the steps, where he landed with a splash in a puddle of questionable origin.

Constance made a final pass, distributing winnings. One man was foolish enough to argue her count, but she poked a knife to his plums, which made short work of the discussion, and he quickly sat, crossed his legs, and made peace with his loss.

Lucas leaned against the bar, murmuring to himself. "So fair of face, so fast and fleet, my heart beats so, I can but bleat." Lucas looked up, blushing as he realized Tom had heard him.

"It's a love poem I'm working on," Lucas said, ducking his head. "For my lady fair."

Constance swaggered up just then, giving Tom the house's portion of the bets. He handed back her cut, which she slipped into a purse in her bosom. Lucas turned scarlet and suddenly felt moved to take a load of dishes to the kitchen.

"Busy night," Constance said, hitching up onto a chair. "Second fight so far. You need to talk to Elsie. We'll run out of bar stools at this rate."

"Yeah, I'll do that." Tom rolled his eyes. "I only just got her to stop using the frying pans."

The Poxy Dragon had lousy beer but good-tasting food, and it was the only tavern in half a league. The regulars came for the food and entertainment and stayed because Tom's whiskey made them too blind drunk to leave. Over in the corner, Benny the bard strummed his lute and cleared his throat, an indication that he wanted his audience to quiet down.

As usual, they ignored him.

He strummed again, a little louder this time. "This is an ode to the heroes of the barren field," he announced.

That got the attention of the closest patrons. Tom signaled to Constance, and she threaded her way with a tray of drinks. Most of the customers hailed her for another round.

"Here's to heroes, brave and tall...here's to heroes, one and all. Here's to heroes when they fall, the heroes of the barren field."

Tom always felt torn on Benny's song choices. Benny had a good voice and still had enough magic now and again that an upbeat song put patrons in a good mood. But a mournful number sold more drinks as he drove them to despair and misery. Constance came back to the bar with an empty tray, and Tom filled it up again as Benny continued.

"Swift were they, their strength to prove...risking all for fame and love...may their souls rise like a dove...the heroes of the barren field."

Tom leaned back, crossing his arms. The whiskey melted more stone cold hearts than Benny's singing, though now and again Tom caught a glimpse of what Benny must have been like when his voice and face won him the devotion of women and the anger of their husbands.

"Sure of might, young and strong...charging in to right a wrong... we remember them in song...the heroes of the barren field." The ballad was long, with many maudlin verses, and Tom was certain that Benny added a stanza or two each time he sang it. He could feel the tickle of magic in the tune.

Tom exchanged a glance with Gunnar, who slid his glass across the bar for another pour. If the song went on much longer, Tom might break his rule and join him.

Constance caught his eye and mimed sticking her fingers in her ears, with her back turned so neither the bard nor the audience could see.

Thaddeus had come in from the cemetery, dirt-streaked as always. He leaned on his shovel, gazing at Benny with rapt attention as the bard sang his favorite song.

Lucas leaned against the doorway to the kitchen, enthralled. Tom thought he could just make out a raspy voice from the kitchen, which meant—gods help him—Elsie was singing along.

Benny's singing was still a wonder when the songs were written by someone else or were the kind of pub ballad that got everyone on their feet, singing and sloshing, arms across shoulders, hail fellows well met. But his new songs were pure shite, filled with pain, longing, and regrets. Maybe that was a sign of what he'd been through. Still, several of the burly men sniffled and more than a few dabbed at their eyes as Benny grew louder, rising to a dramatic finish.

"Beneath the grass, the heroes lie...for fame and glory, they did die...death comes for all, for you and I...all in barren field."

Holmgard, the blacksmith, sobbed openly and raised his glass in a toast. Bjorn, his buddy, clapped a hand on his shoulder in solidarity. Constance had barely gotten the next round sold before the rest of the patrons joined Holmgard in his ceremonial toast, and knocked back their whiskey.

Tom silently reminded himself to have Constance bring around headache remedy for sale before they all staggered into the night.

"Huzzah!" Holmgard shouted, red-faced and bleary-eyed.

"Huzzah!" The crowd replied, sniffling and blinking back manly tears.

Benny managed to look humble and pleased as they threw coins. He didn't even flinch when some of the coins went astray, given the questionable aim of the patrons, pelting him on the shins and knees.

"That was just...beautiful," Holmgard sighed, signaling for Constance to bring him another drink.

Lady Leota sat back in her chair near the boarded over window, hands clasped serenely, gaze distant. Tom never knew whether that meant their resident demigoddess was having a vision or was just exceptionally gifted at tuning out Benny's singing. But if he had to guess, Tom thought she looked like she was expecting someone, and

43

that probably meant a new party of heroes come to test their mettle, may the gods have mercy on their souls.

The door opened, and everyone turned to look as five strangers walked in. The man in the front had dark, curly hair and a fighter's build, tall and strong. Tom figured him for the leader. Behind the first man came a second fellow, solidly built with slate-gray hair and yellow eyes. *A shifter, probably a wolf,* Tom thought, judging from the color of his eyes.

The third newcomer was a woman, with enough elven blood to taper her ears and give her the high cheekbones and unusual eyes common to her kind. Her red hair was plaited close to her head, and her green eyes scanned the crowd for threats. With her was a fourth man with black hair, striking blue eyes, and a scar that ran from eyebrow to chin on the left side of his face. He had a twitchiness to him, but the set of his jaw showed determination.

Everyone noticed the fifth stranger, who cast back his cloak to reveal long, white-blond hair and kohl-rimmed blue eyes. He strutted more than walked, the only one of the five not to appear nervous, and his attention went immediately to Lady Leota, who gave him an appraising look, spared a glance for the man with the scar, and then nodded.

All of the strangers wore cloaks and sturdy boots. They were well-armed with swords, bows, knives, and cross-bows, full quivers of arrows and quarrels, and packs ready for a journey.

"We're here about the quest," the leader said. "We were told there was a contest."

A quiet ripple of laughter ran through the crowd. The leader's eyes narrowed, not sure whether they had somehow become the butt of a joke. "Well? We were told to come to the Poxy Dragon to seek our fortune, and we're here."

"About that fortune..." the silver-haired man added, "we want to know what the purse is before we risk our arses. What's the prize if we complete the quest?"

"Fame and glory isn't sufficient?" Lady Leota asked from her table in the corner. Her unreadable expression gave no clue to her thoughts.

"Hell no, lady," the shifter said. "We can't eat fame, and glory doesn't pay the rent."

The regulars drew back, expecting a rebuff to the newcomer's rudeness. Instead, Leota gave a half-smile, as if the answer pleased her.

"Come closer, my would-be heroes. I want to see you better."

Tom had felt the weight of that one-eyed gaze. Leota's scrutiny felt like she could see down to the bone, cutting through all pretense. He'd heard it said she could see your heart and soul, and maybe as the daughter of War and Memory, and the heiress of Fate, that was true. Now, she seemed intrigued, and slightly amused.

"You, healer," she said to the white-haired man. "Come closer." On first glance, Tom would have said the stranger was beautiful—an odd term to apply to a man, but accurate, nonetheless. One man snickered at the healer's dramatic appearance, but he silenced immediately when the slender man turned a sharp gaze in reply. Something in the man's manner reminded Tom that lovely flowers were often the deadliest.

"M'lady," the healer said, with a courtly bow. The gesture appeared to come by reflex, making Tom wonder if the man had been born to money, perhaps even a title. If so, he'd left it behind him. "What do you ask of me?"

"Who are you?"

"My name is Malyn, and I am a seer of visions and a speaker to ghosts—and yes, a healer."

"Interesting," Leota murmured. "And you? A mage," she mused, taking in the scarred man with an appraising look. "You have power, but it's been broken and reformed. How well? Even you don't know the answer. Do you?"

The man's blue eyes widened. "I'm Declan," he replied. "And all that happened in the past. I'm better now."

Tom didn't have to be a seer to know the mage lied, but then again, Tom had seen plenty of battle-scarred men tell the same untruth.

"It's rare to see a half-elf with humans," Leota said, turning her gaze to the woman. The red-head regarded the demigoddess with suspicion she didn't try to hide.

"It's rare to see a half-elf at all, unless we wish to be seen." She wore tunic and trews like the men, and as with the rest—save for the mage—she fairly bristled with weapons. "We're choosy when it comes to companions."

"That tells me these men have been found worthy of your loyalty," Leota replied.

"Yeah. They have. You, I'm not so sure about. I'm Kane."

"You are right to be unsure, Kane. I'm not at all as I appear," Leota said, though her smile told Tom she was enjoying her game.

Leota's attention turned to the leader and the man-wolf. "The sell-sword and the shifter. Give me your names."

The silver-haired man stiffened at the comment, but the fighter laid a hand on his arm. "I'm Kieron. He's Mitchell. Is it true you have work for us?"

Leota seemed to be enjoying the banter. None of the regulars would dare address a demigoddess so brashly. Even Tom, who had grown fond of the seer, minded his place. Yet these newcomers did not appear to give offense with their candor. Perhaps, Tom thought, Leota tired of so often being told what others thought she wanted to hear.

"You have been betrayed, both of you, and yet honor remains. You tell the truth when you say you do not wish for glory. What, then?" Leota asked, watching the men for their reaction.

The rest of the group looked to Kieron, who cleared his throat. "Enough money to buy a place in the country, where we can live in peace."

Leota canted her head, intrigued. "You don't seek to prove your-selves to be heroes?"

"We're nobody's heroes, lady," Mitchell said. "But when we say we're going to do a job, it gets done. So can we get down to business? Otherwise, it was a long-arse ride for nothing."

"You'll do." Leota raised her chin. "Come closer, and hear your charge."

Kieron exchanged a glance with the others, an unspoken conversa-tion that asked and received assent. Patrons cleared space for them to gather in front of Leota's table, facing the boarded window.

"Long ago, in the kingdom of Sorenden, the first king was granted a boon from a child of the gods." Lady Leota leaned back and crossed her arms. "A wooden crown, cut from a branch of the tree of wisdom, blessed by the goddess of Fate, set with gems chosen to increase insight and courage and enable the wearer to recognize the false-hearted. It served the king and his heirs for generations. And then, in the midst of a bitter war, the king died in battle and the crown splintered."

Leota looked pained, and Tom wondered whether she spoke of the tragedy from memory.

"Without the crown, the new king falters. Great hardship has come to the kingdom. The enemies of Sorenden took the shards of the crown and sent them far and wide, hoping to use its power for themselves. But the pieces do not have the power of the whole. One by one, heroes have reclaimed the splinters of the crown. All, save one."

"I've never even heard of Sorenden," Kieron challenged. "How far is it?"

"Too far to ride. I will send you, and I will bring you home." Leota held up an ornate key on a sturdy lanyard. "This is the passage token. It will return you here, whether you succeed or fail. Use it in any of the lychgates, and it will bring you back—so long as you are all together."

"You still haven't said what the reward is if we bring back the piece of the crown," Mitchell pointed out. "Is this king going to pay a reward?"

"I will reward you," Leota assured him. "Two hundred fifty gelt, fifty for each of you, plenty to buy your land, build your house, purchase livestock and seedlings. Will that suffice?"

"All right," Kieron said. "What do we have to do to get back the splinter of the crown?"

Leota held out a map that Tom knew hadn't been on the table seconds before. "You must travel through the Deadlands, to the Shadow Woods, and from there, to Nightshade Monastery and the Villa of the Commissar, and finally, retrieve the shard from the Crypt of the Renounced."

"Wouldn't it be easier to just start at the crypt?" Malyn asked.

"Those who took the crown and broke it tried to assure it would be difficult to retrieve," Leota replied. "Each location is a piece of a puzzle, and without all of the pieces, you will not be able to free the splinter. In some of the locations, there is a key of sorts that will be needed later. In others, a bit of missing knowledge is what must be gained to go on. Solve the puzzle, find the splinter of the crown, and bring it back to me—and you will have the reward you desire."

Again, the five adventurers shared a look. Declan nodded first, then Malyn. Mitchell chewed his lip for a second, then gave his assent. Kane was the last, and Tom thought the half-elf had a momentary argument with herself before she silently agreed.

"You have a bargain," Kieron replied. He reached out and took the key, settling the chain around his neck. "We'll need provisions, but our horses are ready."

Leota smiled. "You will not need horses. They will be safe here, and well cared for until you return. You may find provisions along the way, but I have some to get you started." She shifted her skirts, to reveal a bulging canvas sack.

"How are we supposed to get there?" Mitchell asked, with a skeptical expression.

"By going through the door, of course." Leota gestured, and where the large boarded window had been, a swirl of color and stars now offered a gateway beyond. "Step through, and you will be where you need to begin. Go with my blessing, my chosen champions. And may the gods go with you."

The newcomers closed ranks. Mitchell grabbed the sack of provisions. Then they joined hands, squared their shoulders, and stepped into the void, vanishing from sight.

5

KIERON

When Kieron and his friends stepped through the portal, the Poxy Dragon vanished, leaving them…here.

"Where in the hells are we?" Mitchell growled, looking around.

"Offhand, I'd say somewhere awful," Malyn replied. "Sorenden, wasn't it? Wherever the fawk that is."

"The Deadlands," Kane murmured. "That's where the quest begins."

Kieron had to admit that their surroundings lived up to the ominous name. This had been a forest long ago. Now, dead trees reached up toward the gray sky like bony hands clawing from a grave, blackened and twisted by whatever befell this barren land. The dead woods stretched as far as Kieron could see. He thought he glimpsed the ruins of houses off to the right, barely more than their foundation stones. To the left, dark grave markers jutted from uneven ground. The air felt stagnant, and although he strained to listen, he could not make out any sounds from birds or animals.

He reminded himself that it didn't mean they were alone.

Kane unrolled the map and studied it. "We're on the Corpse Road," she said, as Kieron and Mitchell crowded closer to see. Malyn and Declan faced in different directions, eyes shut, utterly still. Kieron figured they were using their magic gifts to scan for danger. "Up ahead, we'll have a choice where the road forks. Both take us to the Shadow Woods. One is shorter."

"Shorter is better," Kieron replied. "Especially since we don't know what might be hunting us out here. If it were easy, they wouldn't need to pay us so much."

"In the village where I grew up, the Corpse Road led from town to the burying ground," Mitchell noted. "The elders said that traveling that route protected the bodies of the dead, so their souls wouldn't be stolen or the bodies possessed."

"Did they say it offered any protection for the living?" Kane asked.

Mitchell shrugged. "Not that I remember. I was young. Perhaps I missed that part."

Kieron looked at Declan and Malyn. "Are you picking up anything?"

Declan shook his head. "About the road? No. That doesn't mean that there aren't protections, just that they're not the kind I can sense."

Malyn nodded. "The entire area is barren—not just of new plants, but even the land is sick...poisoned. Whatever sucked the life from this place happened long ago, but I can feel traces of the curse. Whether it is still active, I'm not certain—but I wouldn't suggest we linger."

"How far are we from where the road splits?" Kieron felt jumpy as if his skin itched, and while there was no one in sight, he could not shake the feeling that they were being watched. A glance at Mitchell told him that the shifter seemed equally twitchy.

"Best guess? Not far. But there aren't a lot of landmarks, so I'm not entirely sure where we're starting from," Kane replied. She rolled the map up and smacked Kieron in the chest with it, handing it off. "Here. I need both hands for my bow."

Kieron looked back at Malyn. "Are the ghosts telling you anything?"

Malyn shook his head. "They're watching us, but they haven't decided to come closer. I don't think they're hostile. More like they're trying to figure out who we are, why we're here, what we want. If they decide they don't like us..."

"Well then, we're screwed," Mitchell muttered. "Because our charming personalities got us where we are today."

"Come on," Kieron said, orienting himself on the map from few features he could make out. "This way. The sooner we find the splinter, the quicker we can go home."

"You'd think she could have given us horses," Kane grumbled. "Or let us bring our own. Do we have to walk across the whole fawking kingdom and back again?

"Maybe we can steal some." Declan offered a hopeful smile. "If we ever go near somewhere civilized."

"Can we not end up in jail or hanged for horse thieving?" Malyn targeted both Kane and Declan with his glare.

"I'll make a note of that," Kane replied in a dry voice. But Kieron saw the hint of a smile as she turned away.

Kieron looked at Mitchell. "Any benefit to going wolfie?"

Mitchell rolled his eyes at the nickname. "Keep that up, and my offended wolf will bite you." He looked around at the lifeless landscape and shook his head. "I don't think so, and I'd rather save that for when we need it. Shifting takes energy and requires more food. We don't know how easily we'll be able to replenish the supply the seer gave us. Maybe if we get into a real forest, I can hunt some dinner and sniff out the tracks of anyone who's ahead of us."

"Sounds good. Let's go." Kieron strode off, counting on the others to follow.

The old cemetery Kieron had spotted lay to their left. An iron fence surrounded it, and he wondered whether it was to keep people out—or keep the spirits inside. Where the path to the cemetery led off from the road, the lychgate spanned the entrance to the burying ground, a roofed gate with enough room inside for mourners to sit vigil with an unburied body. The structure looked old, and Kieron hesitated to venture close enough to make out the runes and sigils carved into the wood on the uprights that held the roof.

"They're wardings against evil," Declan said without being asked. "Fairly common outside of the bigger cities. Out in the country, there are still plenty of superstitions about grave robbers and spirits that steal bodies."

"Not all are superstitions," Malyn replied. "There's truth behind the stories. If we have to shelter overnight, we could do worse than a lychgate."

"I'd like to be off the Corpse Road before nightfall if that's possible," Kieron said. He squinted up at the overcast sky, trying to make out the position of the sun.

They had gone to the Poxy Dragon mid-afternoon. But he had no idea whether their trip through the portal happened in the blink of an eye—as it seemed—or actually took time for them to travel such a distance. He hoped that they still had a number of candlemarks until dusk, because the thought of staying in this gods-forsaken stretch disturbed him. Mitchell seemed certain there were no other animals out among the dead trees, but Kieron worried more about what other sorts of creatures might haunt these lands.

Usually when they took a journey together they fell into easy banter and bawdy jokes. Kane and Mitchell's verbal sparring over everything from the weather to the price of eggs was amusing, as when Malyn drew Declan out of his shell by daring him to a one-upmanship on silly rhymes, the dirtier, the better. If something they saw on their trip jogged a memory, Declan often launched into an impromptu lecture, regaling his companions with history, lore, or magical trivia. Kieron preferred sight games, where one person spotted an object and dared the others to guess what it was from the barest of clues.

Those distractions had helped them pass many a long day on the road. But here, no one felt like joking, and Kieron wondered if the others feared, as he did, that any lapse of attention might prove fatal. After all, they only had the one-eyed seer's word for it that they were still in their own world. He'd heard rumors that Lady Leota was a demigoddess or at least a powerful sorceress. Until they knew more about the strange place, Kieron vowed to make no assumptions that things here worked as they did back in Trinadon.

After what he reckoned might have been a candlemark, they came to the fork in the road.

"If the map's correct, it's the only choice in the route between here and the Shadowlands," Kieron said. "Both roads end in the same place. The other way is shorter."

"The map isn't very detailed," Kane pointed out. "We don't know what the long route might be skirting."

"On the other hand, we don't know that there's anything between them, except that maybe they were laid out to go around a farm or a mill that isn't there anymore," Kieron pushed back. His head ached, and he'd was sure that if they could just leave the Deadlands behind, the drain he felt would end. Taking the long route put them all at risk.

"This way," Kieron said, making the decision. "If we hurry, perhaps we can be out of these woods before dark."

The longer they walked along the new road, the more Kieron began to think Malyn's comment about a "curse" had merit. He had felt fine when they went to the Poxy Dragon. Better than fine, because he'd been scared and excited over the chance to win enough money to leave the slums of Kortufan behind.

But since they left the Corpse Road, Kieron noticed a headache that grew from a slight pressure behind his eyes to a steady throb. A glance at the others told them they seemed to be feeling the effects as well. Maybe he could blame the headache on nerves, since they were on their own in a strange place and had no idea what dangers awaited them. But when he looked to Malyn, he saw the healer's concerned expression.

"Do you think something's affecting us?" Kieron asked.

"Maybe," Malyn replied. "It's not direct enough for me to ward against it. If I had to guess, there's a curse on this land that draws out life. That's why there aren't any animals or birds. I haven't even seen insects."

"So we need to get out as quickly as we can," Kieron said. "Maybe when we come back through here, the splinter of the crown will protect us."

"Perhaps. Or we'll be strong enough to withstand the drain, for as long as it takes to reach a lychgate." Malyn paused. "I didn't feel this on the Corpse Road. Maybe we should have taken that route."

Kieron shook his head. "We don't know that it wouldn't have hit us even if we'd stayed on that road. This will get us to the Shadow Woods faster. The quicker we get to the splinter, the sooner we can go home."

Malyn looked skeptical but did not push. Kieron led them on as the dead trees grew taller and more massive, with heavy branches that overhung the road. Kieron's headache had grown worse, and from the pinched expressions of his comrades, he suspected they were all feeling the pain. A question confirmed his guess. Kieron picked up his pace and the others followed.

"I don't think these lands are cursed," Declan said after a pause. "At least, I don't think it's only a curse. Very dark, very powerful magic did this." He gestured indicating the dead trees and absent undergrowth. "Long ago. But the taint remains."

Kieron's nose twitched as he picked up a bad smell. He frowned as he tried to place it, and his heart sank. "Swamp." The sky had grown even more overcast, and the leafless branches overhead were so tight they blocked enough light that Kieron hadn't noticed the wet patches beneath the trees. They came around a bend and found that the path ended abruptly.

"That's not good." Mitchell stared at where dry land gave way to marsh. Dark hulks of rotted trees jutted from water that was dank with algae. Clusters of rushes, sedge, and cattails broke up the watery expanse. A rickety boardwalk dog-legged through the marsh. Even from a distance, Kieron could tell that the structure leaned danger-ously, and the wood was warped and badly weathered. The first several boards nearest the shore were broken. After about twenty yards, fog shrouded the rest of the pier.

"It's a dead end." Kieron's head throbbed in time with his heart. He'd led them the wrong way, in his haste to get to the next part of the quest.

Low growls came from the fetid swamp. At the same time, Kieron felt the temperature of the woods drop and saw mist rise from the ground.

"We need to get out of here," Malyn said, eyes wide. "Ghosts are rising, and *something* is coming out of the marsh."

The short route was a trap—or a test. And I failed. Kieron berated himself, but he couldn't afford the time to think about his mistake.

"Back to the Corpse Road!" This time, they fell into the order they sometimes took on the road when they expected an attack. Kieron and Mitchell in the front, Malyn in the middle, Kane and Declan in the rear.

Kieron had glimpsed the kind of creatures that crawled out of a swamp once before when they had the misfortune to happen upon a couple of ghouls feasting on bodies they had pulled from fresh graves. Leathery, mottled flesh clung tightly to the ghouls' skulls. Their arms and legs were too-thin, skeletal and elongated, almost spider-like, and their bellies were bloated like corpses left in the sun. Long, sharp teeth gnashed behind blackened lips. Ghouls weren't dead, but they weren't really alive. They looked hungry and moved fast.

"We're boxed in," Malyn said in a tight voice.

Kieron looked back and saw the ghostly mist had cut off their retreat, extending far into the dead forest on either side. Going around wasn't going to be an option.

Kane sent an arrow into the chest of the lead ghoul, where its heart should have been. The sharp head went through, sinking the shaft deep into the ribs, with the tip protruding from the back, a shot that should have felled it. Still, the creature came, but now it looked annoyed.

"Take the heads off!" Mitchell yelled, charging forward with his sword ready.

"I'll try to hold off the ghosts," Malyn said. "Take care of the ghouls!"

Kane muttered about wasting an arrow, but she quickly shouldered her bow and drew her sword, as Kieron did the same. Behind them, Kieron heard Malyn speaking in quiet tones, while Declan chanted. Kieron had no idea what the mage and the medium were doing to hold the ghostly threat at bay, but he hoped they could keep that danger restrained long enough for them to fight off the half-dozen ghouls who had crawled from the swamp.

The ghouls must have sensed their advantage, two to one against the fighters. Whatever remained of instinct or strategy paired them against each of the fighters. Kane went after the one with the arrow sticking out of its chest, like that constituted a personal grudge to be set right. It did not seem to expect the ferocity of her attack or her speed.

Kane, sword in each hand, rushed toward the skewered ghoul. Her elven agility served her well as she evaded one attacker's sudden lunge, pivoting to take the head from the shoulders of the other with one blow. She slashed at the second ghoul with crossed swords, neatly decapitating him.

Mitchell relied on brute strength. He brought one sword down at an angle, cleaving the ghoul from shoulder to hip. Still, the creature staggered toward him until his back-swing sent its head rolling. The second ghoul tore at Mitchell's cloak with its bony fingers. Mitchell swore fluently, yanking away from the monster's grip, and drove the point of his blade through the ghoul's gaping mouth and out through the back of its skull, ripping the head from its spine. He shook his sword and sent the head flying into the dark waters of the marsh.

Kieron had his own two ghouls to fight. Their speed and unpredictability made them a challenge. He didn't dare take his eyes off his attackers to see whether more ghouls had emerged, though he could hear the thud of sword against bone and heard the ghouls' guttural cries and maddened shrieks. *If there's anything else hungry out there, it's going to know we're here from the noise we're making.*

One of the ghouls dove toward Kieron, mouth open, going for his throat. Kieron stumbled back, bringing his sword up with a blow that opened the ghoul's belly and sent its rotting entrails tumbling out. The second ghoul saw its opportunity and lunged. Kieron barely evaded the monster's teeth as it snapped at his arm. He rammed a shoulder into the creature and seized the momentary reprieve to swing his sword and decapitate the first ghoul, shifting position to put the body between him and the remaining attacker.

The smell of the marsh warred with the stench of the ghouls' black blood, nearly making Kieron gag. Whatever Declan and Malyn were doing had kept the ghosts from attacking, but the temperature had fallen far enough that Kieron's nose numbed from the cold. The ghoul feinted as if to feast on its downed comrade, then sprang up, almost in Kieron's face, mouth agape and clawed hands outstretched.

Instinct and training took over, moving Kieron's sword without the need for conscious thought. He ducked, blocked, and swung two-handed. The power behind the blow tore the ghoul in half with a spray of ichor. The creature's legs still twitched and kicked, while the hands scrabbled at the dirt. Kieron kicked the skull, tearing it free and sending it flying, and the body fell still.

Ghosts. Still have to deal with the ghosts.

The fight with the ghouls had taken only minutes, though it had felt much longer in the thick of battle. In that short time, more ghosts had risen, becoming an encircling mist that made Kieron's flesh crawl. He could see the strain in Malyn's face and heard the tension in Declan's voice. They couldn't keep the ghosts at bay much longer.

"Switch swords...iron," Malyn said through gritted teeth. "Break through, and we'll lay down a line to hold them. Go!"

At Malyn's behest, they all carried both steel and iron swords, as well as knives edged in silver, save Mitchell. Kieron and the others drew their iron blades and ran forward into the mist, slashing through the ghostly barrier. The clammy air felt like the touch of dead fingers, and Kieron swore that he heard the shrieks and screams of the spirits as his blade cut through the mist.

Malyn and Declan were only steps behind them, sowing handfuls of salt and iron filings across the road and up onto the ground on either side. The fighters' iron swords dispelled the ghosts, and the filings put up a barrier that would at least slow their pursuit.

"Run!" Kieron shouted as soon as they were free of the mist. They sprinted back the way they came, toward the Corpse Road. Kieron and Mitchell made sure they stayed close to Malyn and Declan, in case the ghosts reappeared. Kane forged on ahead, to ensure no new danger awaited them.

Kieron felt the effects of the detour like a fever spreading through his body. His head throbbed, his stomach pitched, and his body felt leaden when he needed agility. While the ghosts did not cross the barrier of the salt and iron and parted before their swords, Kieron could feel their baleful presence and knew the ghosts would take the chance, if presented, to drag them back to the marsh to their deaths.

"Move your arses! Or we'll run out of iron and salt!" Malyn shouted. The Corpse Road lay just ahead, and Kieron berated himself for ever having led them off it. They crossed over and immediately Kieron felt the pressure in his head lessen.

In the time their side jaunt had taken, dusk had fallen. Off in the distance, Kieron saw the foxfire glow of will-o'-the-wisps beneath the dead forest, eager to lead unwary travelers astray. Just as ominous was the unnatural darkness gathering beneath the poisoned trees. Aside from the bobbing orbs, Kieron could make out nothing in the shadows, which seemed far too solid.

Kieron and Mitchell staggered onto the Corpse Road just behind Kane. Declan and Malyn were seconds behind them. The billowing mist stopped at the intersection with the side road, confirming that their initial route conveyed some protection.

"I think the Corpse Road uses very old magic to keep ghosts at bay," Declan said. "I wouldn't bet on it holding off anything else."

"It's getting dark," Kieron said. "We need to make it to a lychgate to be safe for the night."

They pressed on as the sun set, sticking to the center of the road, warily watching the banks and the forest beyond. Kieron and Mitchell kept their steel swords in hand, but their iron blades were within quick reach. Kane slipped her bow strap across her back and switched to the crossbow, better at close range. Declan walked on the left and Malyn on the right, both more attuned to the shadows on their side of the road than what lay ahead.

"The woods were empty all day," Kieron muttered.

"They're not empty now." Mitchell's yellow eyes gleamed in the half-light, and his nostrils flared, picking up scents beyond what humans could detect. "There are creatures watching us, and plenty of ghosts."

Kieron could see the ghosts. The same white mist that had chased them from the marsh rolled alongside the road, never touching the highway itself. Faces appeared and vanished in the mist, some with mouths gaping in silent screams, and others watching in judgment. It seemed to Kieron that the ghosts strained against an invisible barrier that protected the Corpse Road, and if it weren't for the warding, they would have been swarmed.

Now and again, Kieron heard a low growl coming from the

shadows beneath the trees, then a howl. Mitchell shivered and set his jaw.

"Relatives?" Kieron asked.

"Not on the good side of the family," Mitchell muttered. "Whatever packs would live in this gods-forsaken forest would not be happy to welcome strangers. Few packs ever are. But here…more so."

Kieron felt the hair on the back of his neck rise at the sound of a howl that was answered and echoed again and again. As the last hint of light faded, Declan called cold hand light to his palm and Kieron lit a lantern. It made them an easy target, but there was no helping their need for light.

Kane and Mitchell strode forward, able to see well in the dark. "There's a lychgate just ahead," Mitchell called back to them. "We're almost there."

Kieron felt a surge of relief when they crowded into the lychgate's protective enclosure. The dark wooden structure looked to be centuries old, still sturdy, with runes and sigils carved into the lintels and upright posts, as well as on the trusses that held up the roof. The elaborate gatehouse had benches on both sides, *probably for mourners to sit vigil*, Kieron thought. Beyond the lychgate stretched another cemetery marked by more crooked headstones as well as some flat slabs and a few cairns. Kieron spotted more will-o'-the-wisps among the tombs, as well as strands of the ghost mist.

Still, beneath the lychgate, Kieron thought it seemed a bit easier to breathe. Nearly all of the ill effects of the side road had vanished, and he thought his companions looked better as well. Kieron took a lantern from his pack and hung it from a hook on an overhead beam. No one suggested he blow it out, though he did close the shutters on the lamp to make it less of a beacon. He suspected that anything dangerous in the shadows could hear and smell them. Declan set down a perimeter of the salt and iron filings. Malyn and Mitchell dug out provisions from their pack—cheese, rolls, cured meat, and dried fruit, as well as a full wineskin. Kane took first watch, her bow close at hand.

"I doubt there's anything magical about the food, but I think it's the best I've ever eaten," Mitchell said, talking with his mouth full. "I'm hungry."

"If we ration what she gave us—assuming the sack doesn't magi-
cally refill—we should have enough for several days," Malyn said. "If
we get to a place where Mitchell can hunt us some rabbits and there's a
clean well, we might go longer."

"Really hoping we'll be home before then." Kieron studied the
map. They had lost precious time—and nearly their lives—taking his
"short cut." "We have a lot of territory to cover—and we still have to
make it back."

Declan frowned. "I'm not sure that we actually have to retrace our
steps. I think the key she gave us works as a portal." He nodded
toward what appeared to be a keyhole in the lychgate's back upright
post. Kieron hadn't noticed it when he first surveyed the lychgate, but
now that he looked closer, he could see that the key he wore on a strap
around his neck would fit.

"So we can go home from any lychgate?" Kane asked without
taking her gaze off the darkness. The pool of light shed by the lantern
didn't seem to extend beyond the confines of their sanctuary.

"That's what I took from the seer's instructions," Declan replied.

"Me, too," said Malyn. "Although we don't dare test it, and we
could be shite out of luck if we're wrong."

"What else is new?" Mitchell sighed. He leaned back, picking his
teeth with his fingernail.

"We've got trouble!" Kane warned pulling up her bow.

A slim figure strode from the forest. His black frock coat and
leggings over polished black leather boots seemed oddly formal attire
for traveling on foot. Kieron barely had time to register the man's
unnaturally pale face and blood-red lips before Kane had already sent
an arrow flying toward the newcomer's heart.

He plucked the arrow from the air, as effortlessly as if he had
merely caught a fly, and moved in closer to the gate where the sparse
lantern light showed more of his visage.

Vampire, Kieron thought.

"You're new here," the stranger said. His voice felt like honey and
whiskey against Kieron's mind, melodic and enthralling. "Invite me in,
so I can tell you all about this place."

Kieron's logic screamed a warning even as his emotions wanted to respond. Mitchell growled, springing to his feet, stepping close to the edge of their protections and baring his teeth.

"Go away," Mitchell snarled. Apparently his shifter-nature made him immune to the vampire's charm.

The stranger just smiled, but when Kieron's hand went to the silver charm he wore on a chain beneath his tunic, the man's face wavered as if Kieron were seeing two overlapping images. One held the friendly smile and non-threatening expression. But the other revealed a horror —red eyes, sharp teeth, and a cadaverous face. Reflex made him take a step back and grip the amulet tighter.

"We see you as you are," Malyn said, stepping up beside Mitchell, who reluctantly gave way. "You're barely more than a moving corpse, just another kind of leech. Be gone. You have no power here."

The weight of the vampire's gaze fell on Kieron. "Oh, I think you're wrong. At least one of you feels my thrall. Come out, and let me know you better."

His invitation had Kieron moving a fraction of a step in the man's direction before he even realized what he was doing. Mitchell grabbed Kieron's arm with a bruising grip.

"No. Fight the pull," Mitchell urged. Then he moved forward and drew his sword.

Declan chanted. Kane switched to her crossbow and nocked a bolt, one with a silver wash over the arrowhead. Malyn raised his hand, palm out, toward the vampire. A satisfied smile touched the medium's lips.

"Just another dead thing, after all." Malyn leveled a challenging look at the creature. He closed his fingers into a fist, and in the same instant, Kane let her shot fly.

The vampire strained to move but seemed rooted in place. His expression shifted from smug to panicked as he could not dodge the silver-tipped bolt. It pierced his chest, and he screamed, in the seconds before Mitchell's blade sang through the air, slicing his head from his body.

Kieron stumbled back, released from the vampire's spell. The body crumbled to dust, then blew away on the night wind, leaving behind a red gem with an inner light that pulsed like a heartbeat.

Before anyone could stop him, Malyn dove forward, plucking the gem from the dust and retreating within the wardings.

"Why in the name of the gods did you do that?" Mitchell sounded angry. "Something could have grabbed you."

Malyn smirked. "I can see what is—and isn't—in the darkness, just as well as you can. Maybe better." He held up the gem. "This quest took us on our route for a reason. There's likely something in each place that we'll need to get in order to go on. And this gem may be what we needed from the Deadlands."

"What is it?" Kane asked, peering at the gem warily as if it might bite.

"More than a pretty piece of glass—but exactly what it is and does, I'm not sure." He reached into his pack and pulled out a piece of cloth stitched with runes and spells. "That'll keep it from playing any tricks on us, while I figure out what we can do with it."

They were all jumpy after the vampire's visit, but as time passed without another attack, they found their places on the seats or on the ground, agreeing to a watch rotation. Kieron tried to sleep, but he found himself wide awake when Mitchell took over for Kane a few candlemarks later.

"You need to sleep," Mitchell admonished.

"Can't. I screwed up today, nearly got us killed. Maybe you should have let me go with the vampire," Kieron said quietly. He'd gone over his failed decisions all day, angry with himself for disregarding Malyn's advice, for putting his friends in danger.

"Seriously? Get over it," Mitchell said. "We all make shite decisions now and again. Trust me on that—I've done my share."

"I got so focused on getting to the next place on the map, I didn't listen," Kieron replied.

"And the fact that you're not getting a good night's sleep because it bothers you puts you far ahead of my old pack's alpha," Mitchell said. Kieron was grateful his friend didn't turn to look at him. That would have made his confession even more difficult.

"I don't understand."

"One of the reasons I left the pack was the alpha never listened to anyone—and no matter how many times people got hurt because of it, he'd never admit he was to blame," Mitchell answered. "You made a mistake. And you know it. So...do better."

Kieron appreciated his friend's words, but they didn't absolve him. Back in Kortufan, he'd understood the rules. Surviving in the city was a brutal game, but one he knew how to play. Out here, nothing made sense, and he worried that he might not be the best one to lead his party to success.

"We don't follow you because we think you're perfect," Mitchell added as if he guessed Kieron's thoughts. "Because gods know, you're not," he said with a snicker. "But you do the right thing for all of us, most of the time. If you were a real arse, you'd have insisted we keep on going, through the swamp, over that rickety bridge, and probably gotten us all killed. You didn't."

"Still almost got us killed," Kieron grumbled, not ready yet to accept forgiveness. He needed to remember how this felt, incentive not to repeat his mistake.

"And tomorrow, one of us will probably have that honor. When that happens—and odds are, I'll probably be first in line—are you going to leave the person behind to their fate?"

"Of course not."

"And much as it pains me for how loudly you snore, we aren't going to kick you out, either," Mitchell said, staring out into the darkness. "Although I may kick your arse if you keep this up."

"I should have drawn on the strengths of the team, instead of thinking I had to have all the answers myself," Kieron said.

This time, Mitchell did slide a side glance in his direction.

"Sure, when you can. But there's not always time to take a vote. And when there isn't, someone has to just decide. You're the one who brought us together and kept us alive back in Kortufan. I think you're stuck with us, like it or not."

Kieron mulled over his friend's words. He didn't intend to let himself off the hook just yet, but he recognized the wisdom in Mitchell's comments. This quest would confront them with dangers unlike anything they had faced in the city. Like the side road earlier in the day, the quest was a journey. He'd led his companions into danger on a whim, the idea that proving themselves as the champions of a demigoddess might change their fortunes.

And now they were stuck with the decision, despite seeing the reality of just how dangerous their quest might become. Yet none of them suggested using the key tonight to go back. Maybe his dream of a place in the country where they could be safe mattered as much to them as it did to him, something worth risking their lives to win.

Kieron leaned back against the lychgate wall and closed his eyes, drawing his cloak around him. As exhaustion won over recrimination, he vowed to be the leader his friends deserved, even if it cost him his life.

6

MITCHELL

They ate a cold breakfast at dawn, then headed back onto the Corpse Road. By daylight, their surroundings looked far less ominous, but Mitchell and the others had learned the hard way what lurked among the ruined trees, a wasteland that was not as empty as it appeared.

Mitchell watched Kieron, assessing his mood. A few candlemarks' sleep had done him good, and he said nothing more about the problems of the previous day. Declan and Malyn examined the spot where the vampire had vanished, but found only ashes.

His heightened shifter senses were overloaded with the strange smells of the Deadlands, and Mitchell's wolf paced in his mind, wanting to prowl and protect. Kane seemed as twitchy as he'd ever seen her, and Mitchell resolved to know why.

"Tell me what you see," he said, falling into step with Kane, no small accomplishment considering the half-elf set a brisk pace.

She cocked an eyebrow. "I see trouble. Is that a surprise?"

Mitchell shook his head. "Not really. So do I. Just wondering—do we see the same thing?"

Even back in the city, Kane was prickly, by shifter and human standards. Elves usually rubbed folks the wrong way, coming across more often than not as condescending and judgmental. They were an ancient, proud race, with speed, dexterity, and acute senses far beyond regular humans and saw it as a mere matter of fact to say as much.

Kane could be that way, but she also chose Kieron's family of misfits and asked to join. In exchange, she'd pulled her weight, thieving food and coin when money was tight, backing them up without fail in a fight. They all had their secrets, but Kane held her past closer than any of them, and Mitchell could only guess at the tragedies and betrayals that had made her an outcast from her people, on her own in a city like Kortufan.

Kane never stopped scanning the horizon for threats. "If the map's right, we're near the edge of the Deadlands. But what's next—the Shadow Woods—I don't think will be any less dangerous."

"Figured that," Mitchell replied. "If it were easy and safe, the seer wouldn't have had to send in a team of heroes, now would she?"

Kane snorted. "Is that what we are? This is just another job, Mitchell, same as if we'd been hired at the wharves. We're pulling someone's nuts out of the fire, and it'll be a good day if they actually pay us, and we have all our body parts when it's said and done."

"You're not wrong. But you also didn't answer my question."

Kane gave a put-upon sigh, as if the conversation strained her patience. She wasn't one for long discussions on the best day, although she often joined the others for cards, dice, or darts on winter evenings. Now, though, she seemed more unwilling than usual to share her thoughts.

"I don't know," she admitted finally. "And that makes me really uncomfortable. It's like being partly blind, or half-deaf. Either my senses aren't working properly here, or I can't decipher what they're telling me. I can't fight what I can't sense."

"You fired on that vampire last night before any of us quite knew what was happening," Mitchell pointed out.

"But I should have sensed him long before he stepped out of the shadows—and I didn't."

And that's the nub of it, Mitchell thought. Kane relied on her heightened elven abilities, and without that edge, she felt disarmed.

"If it's any consolation, my wolf knew something was wrong, but it didn't recognize him as a 'vampire' right away."

"It isn't."

Mitchell resisted the urge to roll his eyes. "Is there a reason you're making the others run to catch up?" he asked, with a pointed glance behind them. "You and I are faster. They're just humans."

Kane grimaced as if that thought had occurred to her and she found it distasteful. "All right," she said, slowing her pace. The others still had a distance to close to regroup. "Happy?"

"Not particularly, but that's probably not going to change soon," Mitchell replied with a shrug. "What do you think is affecting your senses?"

Kane hesitated, and Mitchell couldn't tell whether she didn't want to admit not knowing, or wasn't willing to share what she did know. "I think Declan's right about this area having the taint of old, very dark, magic. That might be it. But we don't really know where we are. Not in Trinadon. Are we in Sorenden? Or some nether realm of the gods?"

That last possibility had occurred to Mitchell. He'd wondered more when he had overheard Malyn and Declan talking in low tones, a conversation they obviously hadn't wanted to share with the others, or perhaps just not with Kieron. Out of all of them, Kieron seemed to be the least affected by the Deadlands's strange energy. Then again, he was just a human fighter—no magic, no psychic ability, not a shifter or an elf.

"So is whatever's doing this to us intentional, or just an effect of a bigger something that happened long ago?"

"Does it matter?" Kane asked.

"Maybe it does. Because if it's just an effect, then there's nothing personal. It's like having to deal with snow or rain or mud. Uncomfortable, difficult, but part of the landscape. But if it's intentional—"

"Then something or someone wants to keep people from traveling this way, or getting to what's on the other side," she replied. "Yeah. I've thought about that, too. Haven't made up my mind."

"The map takes us to very specific places," Mitchel pointed out. "And the seer said it was all one giant puzzle. Whoever hid the last splinter of the crown went to a lot of trouble. So did they pick harsh landscapes that already existed to make the quest difficult, or create the landscapes to build the puzzle?"

"And I ask again…does it matter?" Despite the edge to Kane's voice, Mitchell could tell she was intrigued.

"If we end up facing off against whoever created the puzzle, it would be nice to know if we're dealing with a master strategist, a games master, or a powerful wizard," Mitchell said.

"Why would a wizard want the splinter? She said that the crown gave the royal family special magic. A wizard strong enough to reshape the land to hide his prize wouldn't need a lucky relic to boost his power."

"Maybe the wizard's master wants the splinter—or wants to keep the royal family weakened and vulnerable. Perhaps it's not so much about hoarding the splinter as it is not allowing someone else to use it," Mitchell suggested.

"You know this is all just blowing smoke until we actually have real information, right?"

"A good strategist plays out all the possibilities before making a move. That way when we do find that important clue, we'll know it when we see it."

Kane's lips twitched into a rare half-smile. "Wily wolf."

"Sneaky elf."

Kane glanced over her shoulder. The others had closed much of the gap, but they were still several paces behind, with Malyn and Declan in the middle and Kieron bringing up the rear.

"You think Declan is up to this?" Kane asked.

"Did we have a choice? We were going out on another job, or we were going to starve."

Kane tilted her head slightly, a tell that Mitchell recognized as a signal she was thinking hard about how to put what she wanted to say in the least offensive language. "He still isn't well. Better—but not well. I know the signs. I've been to war—and lived with warriors. He's mind-scarred."

"Aren't we all?"

"My old fighting trainer used to say, 'it's not the injury, it's how you deal with it.' This quest isn't going to be like escorting a merchant wagon or even breaking into a vault. We've got days on the road, and I think what we've dealt with so far is mild compared to what's ahead," she added. "The pressure is building. I am...concerned...that Declan may not deal with that well."

"Malyn's sticking close to him. And if Declan really couldn't handle it, I think Malyn would have said something to Kieron before we went to the Poxy Dragon."

"But would Kieron have listened?" Kane spared him a pointed glance. Mitchell's thoughts went back to the conversation of the night before. *Maybe? Shite. Maybe not. Was Kieron feeling guilty about more than just taking us on the wrong road? Did he underestimate the danger? Had Malyn warned him and not shared with the rest?*

Mitchell shook his head as if to clear the doubts. "He knows Malyn's protective of Declan. We all are."

"And Declan hates it, for the record."

Of course he did. The mage still had his pride. And he'd come so far from being the frightened, barely functioning man Malyn had brought into their circle. Mitchell was proud of the progress Declan had made, not just in his confidence, but in reclaiming his magic. Though to be fair, not having known Declan before the battle that stole his power and broke his mind, Mitchell didn't really know how close the "new" Declan was to regaining all that he'd lost.

"We've run into bad magic before on jobs. There've been traps in places we've gone to thieve something, and there are monsters in Kort-ufan and the countryside."

"But those jobs were a night, maybe two. This...it's more than I expected."

"We all agreed to the idea," Mitchell said, feeling like he needed to defend Kieron. "No one forced us to come."

Kane shook her head. "No. I'm not saying that. We voted. And you're right—we need the money. Anything we did would have been risky. Fight off brigands, break into a vault, protect someone from hired killers—nothing we do is safe. But this feels..." She let her voice drift off and narrowed her eyes as she scanned for threat. "Do you think that, somehow, the seer manipulated us to come here?"

Mitchell laughed. "How? None of us had ever been to the Poxy

Dragon. Kieron heard about it through pub gossip. How could she possibly know who we even were, out of all the ne'er-do-wells in Kortufan?"

Kane shrugged, clearly uncomfortable. "That pub gossip also said that the seer is a demigoddess. Kieron said she was the child of War and Memory, and that she might even be Fate herself. That kind of magic doesn't work by the same rules."

"Are you asking whether I think the gods chose us?" Mitchell asked incredulously. "If so, they're scraping the bottom of the barrel." He shook his head. "No. I can't believe that. We're just not that special. The gods would have to be quite bored to notice us, down on our luck in the Dregs."

Kane looked away. "I imagine you're right." Her tone said she didn't agree.

"I really hope I am. Because you know what? It's fawking terrifying if what you say is true. I've heard the bards tell stories about people who are chosen by the gods for a great task. It never ends well for them. And personally, I'm counting on moving out to the country to live to a ripe old age. So...screw the gods and their grand plan. I'm pretty sure that my own bad choices got me to Kortufan, and I'd rather believe that than some sort of heroic destiny." Mitchell found himself far more worked up over the idea than he'd intended.

"Then we'll make it up as we go, the way we usually do." Kane's smile had a feral touch. "And may the gods pity any sorry bastards that get in our way."

MID-DAY, the gloom of the Deadlands gave way to sunlight filtering in between the overhanging limbs. Fewer of the big, dark trunks blocked their view, and when they came around a bend, Mitchell saw the edge of the tree line, where a brown stretch of land led down to the river.

"We're nearly out!" he called to the others. Mitchell had never been so happy to leave a forest. Usually, his wolf preferred the woodlands to the crowded city or the open road. But even though he lacked Malyn's ability to commune with spirits or Declan's magic, Mitchell's gut instinct knew that the Deadlands were wrong, an abomination, and contrary to nature.

"Is that a bridge up there?" Kieron asked as he and the others closed ranks around Mitchell.

"Looks like it," Kane agreed. "A fairly big one, so I'm guessing that's the river."

Mitchell shaded his eyes to look toward the far shore. "That river also must be the edge of the curse, or whatever made the Deadlands... dead. Looks pretty green over there to me."

Kane unrolled the map. "If the map is right, the Shadow Woods will be on the other side of the river."

"I'd have said the other side looks rather sunny," Malyn said, squinting at the sunlight after riding so long in the half-light.

"If the gem was what we were supposed to get from the Deadlands, what do you think we might find in the Shadow Woods?" Declan mused. "And how will we know what we're supposed to do with the gem?"

"You're the mage. When you ask questions like that, it really doesn't boost my confidence," Kieron said.

Declan shrugged. "Malyn's the one with visions. I do magic, but I'm not a mind-reader, and I wouldn't look at the future even if I could see it. I've got too damn much to worry about as there is."

The longer they had stayed in the Deadlands, the more Mitchell felt sure the area drained their energy. They still had a long way to go and several challenges to endure before they could complete their quest. He hoped that once they left the cursed land, they would regain that vigor, because he feared the worst was yet to come.

As they continued, Mitchell saw just how large the bridge was, and how wide and swift the river ran below it. Boulders formed the footing, and hewn stones held together two arches that spanned the expanse of water. Mitchell had no idea who had built the bridge, but it had obviously stood for a very long time, maybe centuries, and it looked solid and sure.

"So what's the catch?" Kane asked, falling into step beside Mitchell. "Since when do we just get to walk on through?"

"Gonna cause bad luck, thinking like that," Mitchell chided.

"Don't believe in luck."

"Doesn't mean it's not real."

Kane made a rude noise and edged forward. The others followed. As soon as she was within a few yards of the bridge, three dark creatures burst from the riverbank below. Each had a canine appearance, but was a large as a sow, with squashed faces, bat-like ears, and black, matted hair. They snarled like feral dogs, baring their long fangs.

"Can you turn them away?" Kieron asked Declan.

The mage held out one hand, focusing his power, then shook his head after a moment of concentration. "Not quickly, if I could do it at all. Whatever binds them is an old geas and very strong."

"Are they just beasts?" Mitchell asked. "I mean, can we kill them?"

Declan paused, getting a sense of the creatures with his magic, then nodded. "Yes. I believe so."

"All right, then." Kane readied her bow, and Mitchell and Kieron raised their crossbows. None of them had any desire to fight the creatures at closer quarters than necessary. They moved forward slowly, angling for the best shot. The monsters paced back and forth, growling and snarling, but made no move to charge them.

"I think they're bound to the bridge," Malyn warned. "I'm getting a very strange read—as if they're alive and dead at the same time. Be careful. The standoff may be different from what it appears."

Not helpful, Mitchell thought. Declan and Malyn had told him numerous times that they weren't trying to be cryptic; their abilities just didn't give them all the information. That didn't do much to temper Mitchell's annoyance.

All three of them let fly, and their aim was true. The arrow and sturdy bolts hit in the neck or heart, and the three creatures toppled, blood spurting.

The last length of the road leading to the bridge was badly rutted, forcing them to go single file. Kane was in the lead, and she moved carefully past the still, bloodied bodies. But as soon as she crossed onto the bridge, the corpses wavered as a rippling curtain of energy descended on them. In the next breath, the monsters stood, vicious and unharmed, as if they had never been shot.

"Watch out!" Kane shouted. Mitchell had been right behind her, and only quick reflexes kept him from being clawed by the nearest beast.

"Bollocks!" Mitchell and the others fell back a few paces, and the creatures did not follow, nor did they go after Kane, who remained on the bridge.

"What now?" Kieron demanded as if any of them knew more than he did.

"It's the geas," Declan said after the shock wore off. "They'll only let one at a time through."

"And one person would have trouble killing all three of them at once," Malyn added. "So I think we fire again, and again—getting one person through each time."

"Shite," Kieron muttered. Then he sighed and shook his head. "All right. Let's get on with it. Who's next?"

"I'd say we send Declan then Malyn through, because that puts two of us with bows on this side, and Kane on the bridge, to fire from that side," Mitchell said. "And let's hope that the arrows work from the other side, or we'll end up in a jam."

Kieron shouted the directions to Kane, who indicated she heard and understood. The three raised their bows again and fired. Once again, they hit their marks, and the creatures fell.

"Go!" Mitchell urged as Declan hurried past the dead creatures, picking up the edge of his robe to avoid the blood. The monsters began to stir before he was completely out of range, and Declan yelped with surprise. Kane dove forward and grabbed him by the arm, yanking him past their reach and farther onto the bridge.

"I think they're coming around quicker," Kane yelled back to the group on the other side.

Mitchell growled a curse. "All right. Then Malyn will just have to run."

Malyn glared, but got to the very edge of the safe area, shifting his pack to assure it stayed balanced, then gave a curt nod. "Ready."

The crossbows thudded, and the bolts flew. Again, the creatures dropped to the ground, but this time they did not completely stop twitching.

Malyn had already started running when the shots were fired. He did not slow as he approached the corpses, shifting his path only to avoid the worst of the blood. By the time he had gained more than a step onto the bridge, the monsters had already respawned.

"What if we shot and you shifted, and we ran together?" Kieron suggested.

"I'm faster as a wolf, but I can't shoot and shift, and I can't carry my pack or my clothing," Mitchell said, shaking his head.

"Each time, those things recover faster," Kieron said. "I'm afraid you might not have enough time to get through."

The same worrisome thought had occurred to Mitchell. "What did you have in mind?"

"Put your boots in your pack and give the pack to me. We shoot together, and I'll take your crossbow and run for it. Then Kane, Declan, and I shoot from the other side, and you run across in your wolf."

"And finish the rest of the quest naked?"

"I figured you'd grab your clothes in your mouth if they didn't fit in the pack," Kieron said with a shrug.

"Hurry up!" Kane shouted. The rest of their party waited on the bridge, but Kieron realized that the creatures were venturing farther onto the span with each new trespasser.

"Shite. The longer this takes, the farther those things can wander toward us and onto the bridge," Mitchell said. "I hate to say it, but I think your plan is the best we've got."

He shimmied out of his pack and undressed quickly, stuffing as much as he could into the bag before he helped Kieron shoulder the double burden, as well as his cloak. "Let's hope this works," Mitchell grumbled.

On Kieron's signal, the three fired once more. Kieron grabbed the crossbow from Mitchell and took off running. His long strides crossed the ground quickly, but even so, the creatures were struggling to their feet as he dodged among them. One of the monsters swatted at him with a broad paw with long claws. The claws caught the edge of Kieron's cape and left tatters as they pulled through, shredding the material.

Mitchell tried to quell his nervousness and let his shift flow over him. He howled to let the others know when he had made the transition, then picked up his trews in his mouth and waited for the signal.

The archers fired. Mitchell ran as fast as his four legs would carry him, moving the instant he heard the bows twang. The arrows and bolts hit the creatures, and they stumbled, bleeding heavily, but this time they did not fall. Even in his wolf form, he knew Kane continued to shoot arrows with amazing speed. He heard the thud of the crossbows and hoped his friends' aim was true.

Mitchell's heart thumped in panic. He jumped and sailed over the back of one of the newly-revived monsters, twisting in mid-air as the second creature took a swipe at him. Mitchell felt its sharp claws slide through his fur, scratching the tender skin beneath, a strike meant to rip him open if it had connected with full force.

He landed and slid under the belly of a second beast, evading its teeth and nails as well as the incoming bolt, while making the third creature stop short and tumble over its fellow guardians. Mitchell threaded between the monsters' legs, afraid that he would be easily caught when he emerged.

"Mitchell! Run!" Kieron yelled, and Mitchell glimpsed boots running toward him. Mitchell darted from beneath the creature as Kieron brought his sword down on the beast's neck, severing its head.

"Kieron, get back!" Kane shouted. Mitchell tore over the paving stones as if his tail were on fire. The thud of two crossbows told him that another volley had fired, buying time for him and Kieron.

"Go! Go!" Kieron was right behind him, and a glance over his shoulder told Mitchell that the beasts had gained the freedom to pursue him.

Mitchell practically flew past his companions, intent on reaching the far side of the bridge. Kane moved with elven speed, almost keeping pace. Declan and Malyn were behind her, but the sound of running feet assured Mitchell his friends were moving as fast as they could. Kieron was outrunning the creatures, but it was a close thing.

Mitchell leaped from the bridge to the ground, skidding on loose dirt. Kane and the others jumped the final few feet. Kieron came last, mere inches in front of his pursuers.

The beasts were fast, and Mitchell didn't know how long he and his friends could outrun them. To his relief, the creatures reached the end of the bridge and stopped as if they had hit an invisible wall, shrieking and squealing in frustration.

Mitchell and the others kept running until the bridge was far behind them. They finally stopped, and Mitchell dropped the bundle in his mouth, panting for breath. The others were also breathing hard. Up close, Mitchell saw where the claws had torn through Kieron's cloak, and how near they had come to his flesh. Kane with her elven constitution seemed only lightly winded

"That...was...too close," Declan gasped. Running had never been the mage's best skill.

"Really hoping we don't have to go back the way we came," Malyn agreed, red in the face and puffing like a bellows.

"My arrows did nothing! That many hits should have taken them down easily," Kane cursed.

Mitchell took up his mouthful of clothing as soon as he had caught his breath and padded off to the side of the road. He shifted quickly and kept his back to the others although in the close quarters they often shared, there was little room for modesty. When he had gotten dressed, he returned, and Kieron handed him back his boots.

"At least we know they didn't want the gem," Kane remarked.

"Do you think the bridge was spelled especially for anyone looking for the splinter?" Kieron asked, giving Mitchell his cloak and pack.

"No way to tell," Declan replied. "Although I rather doubt it. I think the magic is part of the curse that made the Deadlands...dead. It felt old, like it had been in place for a while."

"Or perhaps it was cast by someone on this side, who didn't want anything lurking in the Deadlands to cross over and cause problems here," Malyn speculated. "If so, they did a good job of it."

Kane unrolled the map, and they gathered around to see the route. The road appeared to come to a crossroad right before it entered into a large area shaded in pen and marked as "*Shadow Woods.*"

"There's a crossing before the woods, but only this road goes through the forest," Kane noted. "The other two appear to go along the edge, but the map isn't wide enough to show if they actually go around the woods or lead elsewhere."

"While this road does go through to the monastery," Kieron said, regarding the map with a sour expression. "So I guess we don't really have a choice, after all."

Mitchell knew his friend hated the idea of heading into the forest once more, even if these woods appeared to be green and full of life. Mitchell understood Kieron's concern. If the map was drawn to scale, trekking through would require another overnight, and while they still had rations, they would need to hunt or find places to buy food if they finished their provisions before the quest was through, which would slow them down. But there was no way to be sure that either of the other roads would get them where they needed to go, and the woods did appear to be large enough that going around them would be a delay that would cost days.

"Are there burying grounds?" Malyn asked. "If so, then there are likely lychgates, and we'll have a place to spend the night."

Kane pointed to a few indistinct markings. "That's what I think these are. Which means we'll have to decide. If they are graveyards, one is fairly close—we'd probably get there before dark, but we'd give up a few candlemarks of progress. The other is farther away—closer to the other side of the woods. But we'd definitely be walking the last part after night falls."

"I don't like wasting daylight, but I'm less fond of the idea of trekking through an unfamiliar forest in the dark," Kieron remarked. Mitchell suspected that they all thought about the vampire from the Deadlands and the unsettling noises in the night all around their sanctuary.

"I think we're being routed through the Shadow Woods for a reason," Malyn said. "I'd prefer to face that test in daylight when we can see it coming."

Declan nodded. "Night makes some magics stronger, and some weaker. That could work against us."

"We don't know the legends about this place," Mitchell added. "And we don't seem to be running into any other travelers, which worries me."

"Then I think the arguments in favor of stopping at the first lych-gate win," Kieron said. Mitchell hid a smile. He knew that inside,

Kieron was probably champing at the bit to cover more ground, but he had learned from their near-disaster in the Deadlands.

The meadow gradually gave way to scrub, then to forest. Where the Deadlands had been filled with the husks of old trunks and diseased branches, the trees of the Shadow Woods looked healthy and strong, with boughs filled with leaves. *Unseasonably green leaves*, Mitchell realized.

"I don't know where we actually are, but did you notice that it was coming on toward winter when we left Kortufan, and pretty damn cold in the Deadlands, but the Shadow Woods look like summer?" Mitchell pointed out. He looked at Kane. "I thought the elf would have figured that out."

"Half-elf," she said with an eye-roll. "And I'm a city girl. Not all elves commune with nature. Just like not all wolves wear clothes."

Mitchell bit back a smile at their long-running argument. "What do the rest of you think?"

"I fully expect that there's something grievously wrong with the forest, and it'll be filled with dark magic and creatures that want to kill us," Declan replied in a flat voice.

Malyn slugged the mage's shoulder. "Maybe a little less honesty next time?" He closed his eyes, probably listening to the ghosts, or seeking a glimpse of a vision. "Yeah, what Declan said. Nobody in their right minds would go into that forest. It reeks of twisted magic, lousy with angry ghosts, and there are things wandering about that even the spirits fear."

"And it's the only way to get from here to where we need to go," Kieron said, plucking the map out of Kane's hand, then rolling it up and tucking it beneath his vest. "So we'd best get moving. The quicker in, the faster we're out."

Despite the mages' dire warning, Mitchell found his spirits rising as they crossed the meadow. After the dreariness of the Deadlands, he felt the sun on his face and the breeze in his hair. Shifting tired him, but calling out his wolf always felt good. He was surprised that he wasn't hungrier, but figured that the thrill of the fight had deadened his appetite. The wind rustled the leaves in the huge trees ahead of them, and Mitchell remembered how much he enjoyed running in the forest back home, before his relationship with the pack had soured. He sniffed the air…and oddly, picked up nothing but soil and dry grass.

Mitchell glanced at his companions. Kieron looked almost relaxed as he loped along the meadow road. Kane never took her eyes off the woods, but for once her gaze seemed fond instead of wary. Despite her protests, Mitchell felt certain that her elven nature drew energy from a forest, just like his wolf did.

Declan had a distracted look, but the mage often was a bit scattered. Some of it Mitchell blamed on the disastrous battle that had sent him to the Dregs, but part was just Declan, with a mind that flitted from idea to idea. Malyn's expression was harder to read. Mitchell decided not to waste a fine day worrying about it and let himself enjoy the hike.

The meadow ended at the edge of the Shadow Woods. Dappled sunlight reached the ground through the leaves, creating a fascinating, fluid pattern on the ground. The forest beckoned to him, urging him to ignore his worries.

Mitchell didn't realize that Malyn and Declan had fallen behind until he neared the verge of the forest. Just as he was about to step below the canopy, he felt a tingle of magic send a full-body shiver through him.

Just like that, everything seemed different. The scent coming from the forest changed from bark and loam to the heavy smell of rot and sulfur. The leaves overhead were crisp and brown instead of glowing with the green of summer. Behind them, the tall, waving grasses turned suddenly brittle and dry. Mitchell's good mood evaporated, replaced by dread and a cold knot in the pit of his stomach. If he'd been in wolf form, his hackles would have been raised, and his ears flattened.

He saw the utter confusion and disappointment on the faces of Kieron and Kane.

"What happened?" Kieron eyed the forest distrustfully.

"The meadow we walked through put us under a spell," Declan said. "I wasn't sure until just now, and I managed to lift the illusion."

"The ghosts warned me and helped me shake it off," Malyn said.

"They're all around us, deadening its effects to help Declan's magic work against it."

Kieron's expression looked so bereft that Mitchell felt for his friend. "It just seemed like a nice day, after everything we've been through."

"It was a prey spell, wasn't it?" Kane asked, leveling a narrowed glare at the forest as if it were an enemy.

"I think so," Declan replied. "The meadow lulls travelers into a good mood, makes them drop their guard. Then whatever's inside the forest can attack and they probably never see it coming."

Anger at manipulation warred with an irrational sense of loss as Mitchell reconciled his whiplash emotions to the reality of the dark magic. "Do you know what's waiting in there?" he asked.

"Several 'somethings,'" Malyn replied. "But the ghosts aren't very helpful. They didn't see what killed them, or the memories are jumbled."

"The attraction spell, the perpetual summer, and the magic inside— it's like those plants that lure in a fly with nectar and then eat the poor thing when it drowns," Declan added. "But with our wits about us, we shouldn't be any worse off than we are on any other day."

"That's actually not very comforting," Kieron said, grimacing. "All right, then. Stay sharp, and if you start feeling happy—realize it's a trap and ruthlessly squash it."

"I usually do," Kane muttered. Mitchel felt certain that whatever creature had offered her peace and snatched it away would pay dearly.

In the Deadlands, Mitchell felt the energy being drained from him, along with hope and light. The Shadow Woods offered a honeyed trap as if it wished to fatten its offerings before the slaughter. Or maybe, Mitchell thought, just keep them happily cooperating with their own doom.

Now that Declan had shattered the illusion, Mitchell could sense the wrongness in this new place. The trees and plants were a little too perfect, unlike the imperfect creations of nature. As if it had been created by an artist. He reached out to touch one of the trees and found it solid. He didn't know whether confirming that made him feel better or not. The woods were tangible, even if they weren't completely real.

"Nothing is as it seems," Malyn warned. "These ghosts can't follow us. There are other spirits that drive them away. But they've warned us, so we'll have to handle it from here."

Mitchell wondered whether, in his wolf form, he would see the deception more clearly. Then again, his wolf was primal, and while it had the cunning to be good in a fight, it could also be ruled by emotion. No, he thought, better to remain in his human form. Losing the illusion also meant he felt the energy it had taken to shift back at the bridge. He did not want to exhaust himself, or—worse—be unable to shift back if the magic in this place affected him.

"I don't recognize the type of trees," Kane said after they had walked farther. "I've never seen these kinds before."

"I thought the same thing," Kieron agreed. "But we don't know whether that's part of the spell, or because that seer at the tavern magicked us across the kingdom."

Mitchell kept catching glimpses of movement, but when he turned his head, nothing was there. Sometimes he saw shadows flitting across the forest floor. Other times he could have sworn he saw the air itself bend and ripple like it did above hot coals on a fire. Whatever he saw kept pace with them, flanking on both sides, watching. He tensed, expecting an attack. He hated to wait for the strike to come; Mitchell much preferred to take initiative. But neither he nor the others could fight what they couldn't see.

"Stay sharp," Mitchell warned. "Something's out there."

Kieron and Kane checked the map, agreeing that there was still quite a ways to walk to reach the lychgate. Mitchell glanced up, trying to gauge how far the day was gone by the position of the sun, but he found he couldn't quite make it out through the heavy canopy. The dry leaves rustled ominously, no longer the soothing lullaby of warm breezes rustling summer greens.

"Is that a pub?" Kieron asked as a cozy daub and wattle building came into view. The thatched roof looked to be in good repair, and smoke rose from the chimney. The building sat raised on four stout supports in front and back, an unusual construction. A sign swung from a support, reading *Tavern.* The windows held a cheery glow, and the smell of roasted meat made Mitchell's stomach growl.

"Is it safe?" Kieron asked.

"Probably not," Declan said.

"Assuredly not," Malyn replied. "But it's here, and so are we, and we've got no idea what we're supposed to do in this woods other than go through it. So I guess we'll have to go in and see what happens."

Mitchell still felt someone or something watching them, but as he slowly turned to look around, once again he saw nothing.

"Can you feel it?" he asked Declan in a whisper. "Something watching?"

"*Everything's* watching us," Declan replied. "The magic is so thick in this forest, I can't tell what's sentient and what isn't."

Before they ventured toward the tavern, Mitchell and the others checked their knives and swords, reassuring themselves. Kieron led the way, with Declan right behind him. Mitchell and Kane came next, and Malyn insisted on being last, so he could stand on the ladder-like steps and keep watch should an attack come once they were inside.

Mitchell pushed forward for a good look as they stepped through the door. Outside, he thought he had heard the buzz of conversation punctuated by laughter, and he'd thought to see what he could learn from the patrons, since they had seen no one since beginning their quest.

The pub was empty. A cheery fire burned in the fireplace, and the smell of roasting meat and baking bread wafted from the door where Mitchell guessed the kitchen would be. He picked up the tang of dark ale and raw whiskey, mixed with the smell of sweat and dirt from hard-working customers.

"Is anyone here?" Kieron called out.

There were no abandoned trenchers of food on the table or half-drunk glasses of beer. No cards lay scattered, left behind by their owners, and no coats hung from the pegs by the door.

"We need to leave," Kane said, turning and heading toward the exit.

The beams of the pub groaned as the building wrested itself up from where it squatted and rose into the air. Malyn yelped and climbed up the remaining steps, throwing himself inside rather than be left behind or fall to the ground.

With a sound like thunder, the pub took a lumbering step, shaking dust down from the thatched roof. Embers spilled from the hearth and whiskey sloshed in the bottles behind the bar. The tables and chairs slid crazily from side to side with every movement, causing Mitchell and the others to cling to the bar, which was at least fastened to the floor.

"What in the name of the gods is going on?" Kane barely escaped being hit by one of the tables as it careened from one side of the tavern to the other.

"I think we've found one of the magical 'somethings' within the Shadow Woods," Malyn replied, looking more intrigued than panicked.

"Declan?" Kieron called out. Mitchell saw Kieron turn quickly to find the mage who had flattened himself against the wall, obviously trying to avoid the moving furnishings.

"I don't know!" Declan snapped. "I have magic, but I'm not all-knowing! And this...I've never seen magic like this. It's not what they teach in the books. This is old and dark, and oh gods, it's another trap."

Mitchell had already figured that part out for himself. Declan's panic reminded him that despite the brave face the damaged mage presented, the scars from his near-fatal battle were not yet healed, and his magic not completely restored.

"Malyn?" Kieron looked ready to fight; only there was no attacker to confront. Just a moving house that had taken them prisoner, and now carried them off to the depths of a forest dark with dangerous magic.

"No visions, no ghosts. They don't show up on command."

"Can we keep the house from kidnapping us?" Kieron asked.

"Do we want to? There are two men on horseback chasing us," Kane noted, looking through the rear window.

"Shite. Are they chasing us, or the house? And are they trying to save us, or is the house saving us from them?" Mitchell asked.

Declan staggered, and his eyes were glazed, and his face pinched with pain. "So much magic," he gasped. "The house is magic. It's using magic to fight off the men who are chasing us, and they're using magic to stop the house from getting away. I'm...drowning."

A faint blue glow limbed Declan's form, growing steadily brighter until they had to look aside from the glare.

"I said, stop!" Declan shouted, and his cry came with a burst of power that sent them all reeling.

Abruptly, the house stopped and dropped, knocking them all to the floor. Declan looked pale and shaken, but the pinched expression was gone. "Better," he murmured.

"What about them?" Kane asked, glancing out of the window toward their pursuers.

"How did they follow us? Did the seer send them after us?" Kieron asked, ready to fight.

Declan shook his head. "I...don't think so. The forest is magic. It creates what's real inside it. Magic that old and dark might be able to read our fears and serve them up to us."

"Are they real?" Mitchell no longer knew what to believe.

"As real as this house. Real enough to kill us," Declan replied.

"I agree," Malyn said. "The question is—did the forest also make this house, or is there more than one kind of magic—and more than one magician?"

The two men on horseback rode just out of arrow range before they stopped, facing the tavern's front door.

"We know you've got a witch and a wolf in there. Give them to us, and we'll trouble you no more." The speaker was a tall man, dressed all in black, with an odd hat and a grim set to his mouth. His companion looked like a ruffian in a scuffed brown leather cloak with a wolf pelt slung over his shoulders.

"Now what?" Mitchell asked Kieron.

"I guess we fight."

Malyn helped Declan up from where he had fallen. Declan had regained his color and had a sheepish expression. "I'm sorry. I've put my foot in it. It's just, the magic was so overwhelming—"

"There's no telling what the house planned to do with us after it got away from the hunters, so we'd be between the frying pan and the fire no matter what," Kieron said.

"The ghosts outside the forest couldn't enter, but there are more ghosts that belong here. If I can get them to attack the hunters, we'll have cover to leave the pub and get in range to shoot the bloody bastards," Malyn suggested.

"Do it," Kieron replied. He looked around the room. "Where the bloody hell is Kane?"

Mitchell walked through the empty kitchen and found the back door swinging open. A careful glance outside gave the answer. He came back to report. "She went out the back, and she's circling around."

"Shite," Kieron muttered. "All right. Let her do what she does. Declan—do you have your wits about you?"

Declan gave a rueful smile. "As much as I ever do."

"Can you hocus them? If Malyn gets the ghosts to crowd those two hunters closer, and you put a whammy on them to slow their reactions, then Kane and Mitchell and I can take them out with our crossbows. I'd rather not go outside and get into a full fight if we can help it."

Malyn and Declan moved to flank the front door. The cool afternoon had suddenly turned much colder, and a fog rolled in from beneath the trees, billowing around the two hunters. The men's horses shied, distracting both riders as they fought to control their mounts. In the process, the horses scooted forward, closing the distance between the riders and the pub. The spirits shrieked and moaned, setting up an awful racket.

Declan swung into the doorway and sent two streams of blue fire lancing across the distance, aimed for their attackers. Mitchell and Kieron fired their crossbows, and a second later Mitchell heard the twang of Kane's bow.

A silver light flared, repelling the arrows and bolts and sending them back toward the pub. The shielding also deflected Declan's blue fire. One of the fire streams hit the outside wall of the pub, leaving a deep hole. The other came right for Declan. He threw up a defensive shield seconds too late and dodged out of the way of a strike that burned past him and blasted into the plank flooring, leaving the wood smoking.

Distracted by Declan's strike, the witch-hunter couldn't deflect a simultaneous magical and physical attack. Sweeping away Declan's salvo meant that Kane's arrows hit their marks, one in the arm of the wolf-finder, and the other in the hindquarters of the witch-hunter's horse.

Mitchell and Kieron readied another round of bolts, as Malyn coaxed the ghosts to cooperate. Declan made a ripping gesture, and the air above the two hunters parted to release a swarm of buzzing locusts. Both of the attackers were momentarily overwhelmed as they flailed at the air around their heads to see their way clear.

Declan's magic was practical, brilliant, and unpredictable. Mitchell didn't know if that was because the mage was a genius at doing the unexpected, or if his damage sometimes jumbled his thoughts and scrambled his strategy. Whatever the reason, the sheer surprise of his attack gave the others the opening they needed.

Mitchell and Kieron shot again, and this time Kane's arrows came from a different angle. The witch-hunter managed to pluck one of the shafts out of the air. A second arrow grazed the man's shoulder, and a third shot went wide.

A green streak of power lit up the doorway, throwing Declan across the room and against the wall hard enough that he did not get back up. Glowing green tendrils of energy sparked up and down the mage's body, and he shuddered and convulsed, eyes wide and mouth working like a fish out of water.

"Help him!" Kieron snapped. Malyn was already on his way, kneeling beside their friend.

The next magic strike lobbed a ball of flames into the thatched pub roof, which caught like tinder. Smoke wafted down into the common room, along with burning embers. "We've got to get out!" Kieron shouted.

"They'll kill us if we leave the pub," Mitchell argued.

"We'll burn if we stay."

Mitchell felt his anger reach the boiling point. First, Declan struck down, now his friends endangered, all over magic and because of him. With a growl, Mitchell called his wolf and bounded for the back door of the tavern. Stripping off his clothing as he ran.

"Mitchell!" Kieron yelled after him, but Mitchell was too far gone in his fury and his need to avenge Declan's injury. He glimpsed Kane beneath the tree line, and she shot off two arrows with her longbow, one of which was thrown aside by a gesture from the witch-hunter, and the other caught the wolf-finder in the back. The man gurgled as the shaft pierced his lung, and then slowly topped from his horse, bleeding from the mouth.

His body vanished before he hit the ground. Mitchell growled and turned his focus on the other man, running headlong at the witch-hunter. The memory of Declan on the floor, writhing beneath the green energy made him seethe with the need for vengeance. More arrows sang through the air, and Mitchell sprang at the witch-finder in the seconds his attention was required to keep from being skewered.

They crashed to the ground together, with Mitchell's weight keeping the slightly-built man pinned beneath him. Mitchell lunged for the throat, jaws wide and teeth bared.

The witch-hunter vanished from beneath him. Mitchell snarled and dropped to a crouch, scanning the area. He saw the hunter appear halfway across the meadow. His wolf was in charge now, full of rage and the need to kill the threat to his family, his pack. He coiled, ready to run after the hunter and finish the job.

"Mitchell. Stay," Kieron yelled from the doorway.

A clap like thunder rang through the meadow, and a short, squat woman with steel-gray braids appeared in front of the tavern. She waved a hand, and the fire that encroached on the pub's roof went out. Another gesture repaired it as if the fire had never happened, and fixed the hole in the wall as well.

Kieron burst from the doorway, running toward Mitchell. Kane remained in the trees, wary of the new arrival.

Mitchell had obeyed Kieron's command, and when he looked back, the hunter had disappeared. He lifted his head and howled his frustration, still tensed to pursue his prey.

"Chase him, and we lose the quest," Kieron challenged. "Mitchell, you've got to let him go, or we might all die here. I'm not sure that he's even a real man and we need the group—the whole group—to succeed."

Mitchell glared at Kieron and protested with a whine and several sharp barks that made his opinion clear. Still, enough human reason remained to override his feral nature. With a huff, he gave a shake and then turned to size up the newcomer. Mitchell lowered his head and growled.

"Stop that," the woman snapped. With his heightened shifter senses, Mitchell could make out a faint glow around the stranger, telling him that she, too, was a magic-user. His senses couldn't assure whether she was friend or foe, and he wasn't the trusting type.

"I could have killed you all if I'd have wanted to."

The woman was plump and looked like she was accustomed to hard work, with a practical dress and a stained and worn canvas apron. She wore sturdy boots and had sigils inked into her skin on both arms. A glowing crystal hung on a strap around her neck.

"What do you want?" Kieron turned to face the woman, putting himself in between her and Mitchell, who was still in wolf form.

"For one thing, to get away from those odious sendings," she replied with a sniff. "Although they came looking for you. Looks like the forest is up to its old tricks."

"Who are you?" Kieron demanded.

She chuckled. "Names have power, don't you know that? Lady Brewer will do. This is, after all, my pub."

"What do you want with us?" Kieron's fighting skills might not be a match to her magic, but the stubborn look on his face indicated he would go down trying.

Lady Brewer regarded him, arms crossed over her chest. "I wished to see how you would react. The two hunters were none of my doing, but they still served the purpose. You did not leave your hunted friends behind."

"Of course not," Kieron snapped. "But we have a job to do, and those hunters hurt Declan. Can you help him?"

Lady Brewer nodded. "If he is physically damaged more than your healer can fix, I will try. His mind, and the old scars he bears, even I cannot repair."

"And the tavern? Having a building get up and move?"

She smiled. "It pleases me. Only the brave or the foolhardy come through the Shadow Woods. They see in my house what they wish to see, and I see in them their true nature. If I approve, I let them live, and aid their quest. And if not—" Her shrug finished the sentiment eloquently.

"And what about us? Did we pass?"

Lady Brewer tilted her head. "Yes," she said after a worrisome pause. "You did. You tried to defend my tavern as well as your friends, and you did not think to rob me when you did not see anyone inside. Tell me your quest, and if it lies within my ability to do so, I will help."

Kieron looked to Mitchell, and Mitchell let go of his wolf, shifting back to human. His clothing was inside the pub, and he walked back with the others, defiantly naked. No one seemed to care. Kane finally came out from among the trees, but she hung back, still wary. Lady Brewer gave her a nod of acknowledgment but did not appear concerned about either the half-elf or her bow.

By the time they went back inside the tavern, Declan was awake and sitting up. Malyn hovered over him, with a worried expression. Declan looked pale and drained, but at least none of the bright green energy tendrils buzzed up and down his body.

"So damaged, for one so young and powerful," Lady Brewer murmured, coming to stand beside Declan. "I could protect you. Stay here in the Shadow Woods, in this house, and the things you fear cannot touch you."

Declan shook his head adamantly. "No. I go on with my friends."

Lady Brewer raised an eyebrow but nodded as if she was not wholly surprised. "Very well. I will heal the rest of the damage the weed spell caused."

"Weed spell?" Malyn asked, eyes narrowed.

"A garden loses its vigor to the weeds," she replied. "A weed spell sucks away magic the same way weeds take away the life of the soil." She stretched a hand over Declan, palm down, fingers splayed, and spoke a word Mitchell did not quite hear. Declan stiffened, then relaxed, and the tension in his face eased.

Malyn did his own evaluation, letting his hands skim down Declan's form without touching him. He looked up, then nodded. "He's much better. Thank you."

Lady Brewer favored Malyn with a knowing smile. "He is restored to the condition in which he entered my tavern. No more, no less. He should rest a moment and eat before you move on."

Mitchell found his discarded clothing and weapons and got dressed while everyone's attention was on Declan. He hefted his crossbow over his shoulder and turned to face their host.

"What about our quest?" Mitchell asked, and forced himself to meet the witch's gaze.

"Brave little wolf, aren't you?" she replied. "You've come for the splinter of the crown."

"Does everyone who comes this way?" Kieron asked.

Lady Brewer let out a belly laugh. "Gods and goddesses, no! I was warned you might be passing through, and what you came to find."

"The seer." Kane's flat tone conveyed her mistrust.

"Oh, Leota is far more than a seer," Lady Brewer said. "So much more. But yes, she told me of your quest, asked me to determine your suitability, and help you along if I approved."

Lady Brewer turned to the table, and within the blink of an eye, trenchers of food, and drink appeared. "I promise you it is safe and puts you in no debt to me. Please, before you continue your quest."

Mitchell only debated for a moment before taking a seat and filling a plate. The shift always made him hungry, and the food Lady Brewer set out smelled amazing. The others slowly joined him.

"We have a map," Kieron ventured, looking carefully at the food as he sipped the ale. "What else do we need to know, that isn't on the map?"

"More than I have time to say," Lady Brewer replied. "But heed well what I tell you. The token you obtained in the Deadlands will open a door for you. Don't squander it before its rightful use. Your map shows a route, but not where to go once you arrive." She reached into a pocket of her apron and drew out a piece of parchment wrapped around an old key, then set the bundle on the table beside Kieron. Everyone watched as he carefully unfolded it.

"It's a floor plan. And another key."

"For the place you are to go next," Lady Brewer said. "Study it well. Consider your path very carefully, and do not get distracted. Take only what you were sent to find."

"Thank you," Kieron said, placing the parchment in a pouch on his belt. "Can you tell us anything of the road ahead?"

"Do not travel the Shadow Woods by night," she warned. "They are not for the living. The first lychgate is not far ahead. Stop there, and resume your journey in the morning. Do not trust anyone you meet on the road. This woodland is full of traps for the unwary."

"How do we get back to the Corpse Road?" Kane asked, still looking unconvinced as she picked at her food. "Your house carried us off into the forest."

"There is a protected path, straight out of the tavern's door. Follow it, and it will bring you back to the Corpse Road. Do not leave the path, no matter what you see or hear. Nothing outside the path can hurt you as long as you do not leave the trail."

Malyn helped Declan to his feet. The mage looked shaken, but otherwise, much improved. The meal and ale seemed to have brought some color back as well. Mitchell knew how much better he felt and Declan had certainly been in worse shape than he.

They thanked Lady Brewer once again and headed out toward the trail through the forest. Kieron and Kane were in the front, with Declan and Malyn in the middle, and then Mitchell, guarding the rear.

Malyn had dismissed the ghosts he summoned to help fight the hunters, and Mitchell did not sense ghosts near them now. He thought that having the spirits accompany them as far as the Corpse Road might not be a bad idea, but something held him back from asking.

As much as they might have liked to discuss what they had just experienced at the tavern, no one spoke on the trail. In the Deadlands, Mitchell knew that restless and vengeful spirits lurked all around them, and the energy drain made the journey grueling. But here in the Shadow Woods, reality itself seemed unstable, beyond what mere magic could achieve.

As they moved through the forest, Mitchell felt certain they were again being watched again. He wondered if the witch-finder was back, but as he scanned the area, he didn't see any creatures. What he did see caused him even more concern. The land around him constantly changed, from one glance to another. Even if he stood still, to avoid a trick of the light or the angle of sight, trees rearranged themselves in the time it took to blink. Rocks and hills moved. Never when he was watching them, but when his gaze shifted, or he could not refrain from blinking, the woods were slightly altered when his focused returned. He tried to catch the forest at its magic, but the best he could manage was a bit of blurry movement out of the corner of his eye.

What would happen to anyone foolish enough to step off the path? Nothing good, certainly. Mitchell felt sure that he caught whispers and grumbles just at the edge of his sensitive shifter hearing. Creatures followed them, ready should they make a mistake. Perhaps the Shadow Woods were untethered in time and space, as he had heard some unlucky wizards became when they attempted forbidden spells that outstripped their abilities.

There were magics, shadowy and questionable, that permitted the mage to cross great distances, move forward or backward in time, or explore hidden worlds. Sometimes, the mages arrogant enough to attempt such journeys became stuck, or lost their physical bodies or even their souls. Maybe such doomed and damned creatures were welcome in the Shadow Woods, since it did not welcome those still among the living.

The path through the forest took longer than Mitchell expected, and he hoped that they were wise to trust Lady Brewer. Then again, striking off on their own would have hardly been a safer—or saner—choice. It did not escape his notice that his companions crowded together, shoulder-to-shoulder in the center of the trail when the path was wide enough for them to spread farther apart. By the time they had gone far enough that the tavern was out of sight, the five were practically on top of each other.

Voices from the forest whispered in Mitchell's mind, urging him to shift, to leave his human side behind and lose himself in the woods. Howls and yips from deep inside the forest made his heart ache for his old pack. Other voices promised him revenge on those who had taken his pack from him, killed the people he loved, driven him away. Their words stirred his blood, and he fought not just against the voices, but against his own deepest desires.

Either the forest's twisted magic could read Mitchell's mind, or it merely urged his darkest dreams to the fore. He saw the alpha who killed his father and brother, saw the faces of the tribunal members who believed the killer's story over Mitchell's, and the shame and disgust in the faces of the rest of the pack members as they turned away, leaving Mitchell to his fate.

He'd escaped their death sentence, and run to Kortufan, losing himself in the city, largely denying his shifter side—and nearly dying in prison, where Kieron found him. Mitchell told himself that the years blunted his grief and rage, but he knew the truth, that it had never gone away.

Now the voices promised him not just resolution but the revenge he'd seen in his fantasies, humiliating the proud Tribunal for their mistake—or corruption. Proving himself to those who scorned him. And most of all, killing the man who took everything from him, making him pay.

Mitchell hadn't felt the pain this sharply in years, strong enough to make him choke back a gasp. His mind clouded with rage, and his heart felt as if it would shatter all over again from loss.

I thought I was past this. I thought I'd accepted it. I thought I'd left it behind me.

And then, just when he feared he might actually tear free from his friends and run for the forest, the pain brought an instant of clarity.

I can't change what happened. I can't bring them back. And even if I could, I don't want to go home.

"I...refuse," Mitchell grated through clenched teeth. His chest tightened with grief, and his throat nearly closed with emotion, but he held tight to the pain, letting it burn through him like a wildfire, purifying and terrible. He felt it like he had never let himself fully feel before, not just the pain but the loss, and more than that, its finality.

"It's over." Not forgiveness, not by a long shot. But for the first time, acceptance. In that moment, the voices went suddenly silent.

Mitchell felt Declan stumble beside him. He would have fallen without support from Malyn and Mitchell. "Sorry," Declan mumbled. His eyes shone with unshed tears, and Mitchell wondered what honeyed words the forest used to sway him. Declan had told them only a little about the disastrous battle that left him a scarred shell of his former self. Mitchell didn't doubt the seduction of promises to make him whole again, even if those promises were lies.

"Don't listen," Mitchell said, gripping Declan's arm more tightly. "They can't give you what you want."

"Maybe they can." Mitchell and Declan both turned to look at Malyn. Strain and sorrow marred the healer's beautiful features, and the look in his eyes was bereft. "They could make me believe it was all true," he said in a tight voice, just above a whisper. "If the lie is good enough, you stop looking for the truth."

"Fight back," Mitchell snapped, as much to convince himself as the others. "I want what they're offering me so bad I can taste it. But it's not real." He turned toward the forest around them. "Do you hear me, you invisible sons of bitches? We know you're lying!"

Mitchell looked past Kieron and Kane, who were clinging to each other with a white-knuckled grip, fighting their own desperate battles. "I can see the Corpse Road! We're nearly there. Bollocks and balls! We didn't come this far to go down without a fight. Almost there!"

In the end, Mitchell ended up shoving at Kieron and Kane to make them move and dragging Declan and Malyn with him. They stumbled through the intersection like sleepwalkers, and Mitchell thought his companions acted as if they'd been drugged. *Maybe we all were. Maybe that's part of the trap.*

As soon as they crossed over onto the Corpse Road, the last trace of the voices vanished. Mitchell fell to his knees, splaying his fingers wide over the surface of the road, glad to have the slightly stronger protection from the woods. One by one, the others followed his lead. Kieron and Kane looked confused, but Malyn's somber gaze held understanding, and Declan's expression was one of surrender.

"We're out of their reach here," Mitchell said, feeling as tired as if he'd run the whole way. "Come on. Get your heads clear. We've got to get to that lychgate before dark."

7

KANE

EVERYONE BREATHED EASIER WHEN THEY REACHED THE LYCHGATE IN THE Shadow Woods, even Kane, although she didn't let it show. She had insisted on taking point, arguing that even a half-elf was faster than a human, and Mitchell had already exhausted himself by shifting.

Scouting the road kept her mind too busy to dwell on the bigger quest, or what they'd survived thus far. Being the scout meant staying completely in the moment, senses on high alert, with no opportunity to become distracted. Kane needed that focus, because her thoughts, when she would finally be forced to return to them, were a disquieting mess.

"There it is." She saw the lychgate on a slight rise ahead and restrained her instinct to run for shelter. Instead, she sauntered, doing her best not to think about how the forest made even the strongest among her companions nervous and jumpy. While the Corpse Road may have given them more protection than the path, the Shadow Woods still taunted them and whispered.

Still, she couldn't deny how good it felt to step into the lychgate's magical zone of protection and out of the constantly shifting energies of the Shadow Woods. Even here, Kane was not fully off her guard, but then again, that was true no matter where she went.

"I can't wait to be out of this forest," Kieron said as he dropped his pack and found a place on the ground beneath the lychgate's roof. Unlike the first gate where they had taken shelter, this was designed with walls made from intricately carved wood on two sides, leaving the front and back open. But the gate's powerful wards formed a barrier all the same, and the energy inside felt clean and light. It made Kane feel as if she had rinsed off a layer of mud and sweat beneath a pristine waterfall, invigorating her senses and clearing her mind as well as purifying her body.

"If we leave here once it's full light, we should be to the other side by midday," Mitchell said. He walked to the back of the gate and looked out into the graveyard behind the shelter. A stone temple rose at the far end of the cemetery, but at this distance, Kane couldn't figure out to which god or goddess it was sacred.

"Can't be soon enough." Malyn helped Declan shoulder out of his pack and made sure he was seated comfortably on one of the benches. His glare and body language waged an unspoken argument to examine Declan's injury, which Declan ultimately lost. Declan looked put-upon as the healer checked him, giving in to Malyn's implacable will.

"How is he?" Kieron asked, directing his question to Malyn.

"What Lady Brewer did appears to have worked," Malyn replied, although the consternation on his aristocratic features suggested that the truth might be a bit more complicated. "I won't trust anything to be as it appears until we're free of this place."

"You don't have to feel the magic turn itself inside-out." Declan looked haggard, more than Kane would have expected if the pub witch's healing had been thorough. "It folds and spins my energy with it, or would if I let this bloody place into my head. Even so, it's like being inside a ball of dough when it's being squeezed and drawn out, and everything you think is real changes."

"I don't envy your magic," Mitchell said matter-of-factly. "My shifter sense can't make heads nor tails of what I smell and see here."

"I can sense ghosts in the graveyard," Malyn said, looking out over the burying ground with a pensive expression. "But even they seem to be affected. Their energy is…disrupted. Like someone waving a hand through a plume of smoke. It's still there, but not as it should be. I don't dare listen too closely. They're trapped here, and their cries would surely drive me mad."

"I was going to complain that I had a horrible headache and my stomach feels like I've been spun in circles, but maybe being human without any special talents has its advantages. I think I've come out ahead, this round," Kieron remarked.

"It's as if my hackles should be up," Mitchell complained. "It feels like having your fur rubbed in the wrong direction and hearing a loud screech." He shook his head as if to clear the sound from his ears.

"What about you?" Malyn's gaze always made Kane feel like he could see down to her bones. She didn't dislike Malyn, but his psychic abilities unnerved her. Declan's power was unlikely to strip her secrets bare, but she always wondered how much Malyn could see of what she wanted to stay hidden.

"I don't like this place," Kane admitted with a shrug. She looked away, hoping to sound off-handed. "It jangles my nerves."

That understated the discomfort she felt. Elves were attuned to nature, far more so than humans. The wrongness of the Shadow Woods thrummed through her veins, resonating like a discordant song. It took effort to concentrate, since the jarring energy of the strange forest made her thoughts scatter. Kane blamed her human side but had to admit that even a pureblood elf would not be immune to the Shadow Woods's effects.

Declan stared morosely at the keyhole in the lychgate's back pillar, which would take them home, or so they'd been told. Kane had never envied his magic, and the idea of feeling the strange, twisted power of the forest even more strongly made her ill just to think about it. Declan didn't complain, but he looked utterly miserable, and she felt certain that he would rather be anywhere else but here.

"The Corpse Road ends where we cross the border out of the Shadow Woods," Kane said. She had studied the map and committed it to memory. The training she'd received from her father's people—before the elves had cast her out—focused on wood lore and tracking. Those skills served her well in most places, but the Shadow Woods operated under different rules. Perhaps her senses wouldn't be quite so compromised once they left this awful place.

"Is that a good thing, or a bad thing?" Malyn asked. "After all, the road kept a lot of bad things at bay, both in the Deadlands and here. I hate to think what it would have been like if we had to hold all that off ourselves."

"Not sure," Kieron admitted. "It might mean that the next area isn't twisted or cursed. If so, then it shouldn't be any worse than getting around Kortufan."

"I got stabbed the last time I traveled around Kortufan," Mitchell pointed out. "So if that comment was meant to be reassuring, you missed the mark, mate."

Kieron rolled his eyes. "You know what I meant."

Mitchell dug through the pack of provisions that Lady Leota had given them at the Poxy Dragon. It continued to supply their needs, and none of them were willing to look too closely, lest they jinx the magic. Bread, dried fruit, cheese, and sausage sufficed to provide a meal, if not a feast, and neither the wineskin nor the water skin had gone dry. The warm food at Lady Brewer's hut had almost seemed like a feast in comparison. Kane wondered if they could keep the seer's gifts when they returned. All of them had gone hungry far too many times to take a steady food supply for granted.

Malyn helped Mitchell distribute the food, and they ate in silence. Kieron lit a lantern, and hung it from a hook, shuttered to provide light without being bright enough to reveal them. When they finished eating, Declan withdrew a length of rope from his pack, which he carefully curled into a large spiral. The mage anointed the rope with salt and then sprinkled it with blessed water and oil, invoking protective magic.

"I'm going to lay the rope on the ground around us to make a warding circle," Declan said. "It should reinforce the protections of the lychgate, and might give us all more peace to sleep."

They might have dozed last night, but everyone confessed that their dreams were uneasy. Since the most challenging tests of their quest still lay ahead, Kane wouldn't object to even a few good candle-marks of sound sleep.

"I think two people should be on watch at all times," Malyn said. He stretched like a cat, rotating his shoulders and angling his neck to ease tense muscles. "That way if the energy of the forest begins to affect one, the other can intervene."

"Agreed," Mitchell and Kieron replied.

"We should go as soon as it's full light," Declan warned. "We don't dare try before that, but we shouldn't linger. The forest might make it difficult for us to leave."

Kieron and Mitchell looked at the mage in horror. Kane felt a chill go down her spine as Declan said aloud something she had secretly found worrisome. Malyn didn't look surprised, and she suspected his psychic abilities and connection to the ghosts gave him insights into the forest's unstable nature that the rest of them would sleep better not knowing.

"You think it will try to stop us from leaving?" Mitchell asked. He had tensed, and Kane knew the wolf in him was ready to battle an opponent, but there was no physical enemy for him to fight.

"I think it's a possibility," Declan replied. "We haven't passed any other travelers. If there's a way to go around these woods, I'm sure those who live in this area do so. The energy here is damaged. I think that if the forest succeeded in luring us off the road, it would drain us to try to stabilize itself."

Kane hid a shudder at that thought. "I'll take first watch," she volunteered.

"I'll join you," Malyn replied

The remaining three members of their group huddled together in the center of the lychgate, trying to be as far from all the walls as possible. Malyn laid down the blessed rope to encircle them, but that meant whoever was on watch was outside of the extra protection. Kane took a position looking out toward the road, while Malyn found a place where he could watch the graveyard.

The group fell silent as those off duty struggled to sleep. That left Kane alone with her thoughts, without the distraction of the road. Beyond the lychgate's protections, the forest shifted and twisted, sending off unquiet energy in waves. Humans sometimes talked about finding peace in the woodlands, but their limited senses meant they perceived a fraction of the connection elves took for granted.

No one, human or otherwise, would find the Shadow Woods peaceful.

Kane turned and glanced at Malyn, without being obvious. Kane had fallen from high status herself, so she read the tells that Malyn couldn't completely hide. Back in the city, despite their reduced circumstances, Malyn always looked impeccable, favoring brightly colored fabrics and good cloth, even if it was threadbare with wear.

Like her, Malyn could pass among those of means without drawing attention, and when the two of them had worked a job like that together, Malyn gave more of himself away than he might have realized. She didn't know what had led him to the Dregs of Kortufan, whether it was a rejection of his magic or the penalty for his refusal to conform, wearing what he pleased and presenting himself as he chose.

For that, Malyn won Kane's grudging regard. And like her, his slight stature didn't stop him from being a fearless fighter when circumstances demanded. She'd seen Malyn stare down much larger opponents with sheer strength of personality, and wield the intimate knowledge gained from his psychic abilities and his gift of talking with ghosts as a finely honed weapon. He pretended to be aloof, but she saw how he worried over Declan, who was both the most fearsome and most vulnerable.

Kane had chosen Kieron and Mitchell for her cohorts in crime because beneath their rough exteriors, they had a basic decency that was difficult to find anywhere, but more so in Kortufan. And in the halls of the elven princes, Kane thought bitterly. She'd found little enough decency among her people when her parents were murdered by her father's brother, and none at all when she avenged them and they'd cast her out rather than acknowledge the truth.

Malyn and Declan had that decency as well, hidden under layers of sarcasm in Malyn's case, and buried in the shards of a damaged psyche for Declan. Kane watched Declan's uneasy rest. His eyes always had a haunted look, and she knew he faced the ghosts of memories that lay beyond Malyn's abilities to see.

Kane's watchful gaze scanned the restless forest. Even within the safety of the lychgate, she felt reality twisting and folding as its fractured energy juddered. That unstable power was likely to tear apart any living thing that blundered into it, which meant that the creatures whose cries filled the night had strange magic to enable them to survive. She doubted that they would be pleasant to encounter.

Time and again her attention returned to the keyhole. They could call the whole quest off and go home, return to their miserable hovel in the Dregs, and trust that they could steal enough to make it through the winter without falling afoul of the constables. Or they could go on against the odds, and if they survived leave Kortufan behind them forever.

Kane had joked about Kieron's dream to buy a place in the country where their own mismatched "family" could be safe, no longer worried about constables, hunger, or cold. She hadn't wanted the others to see just how much she wanted that dream or to admit to herself how invested that made her in this crazy quest. She'd relied on no one but herself before she had teamed up with Kieron and Mitchell, and it had served her well. Even in Kortufan, she often ran her own schemes, bringing back the money to the group but operating on her own.

This quest required cooperating, something that made her uncomfortable. So far, they'd worked together well. That still didn't make it easy.

"What's your plan once we get to the monastery?" Malyn asked. It had grown so quiet, his voice made her jump.

"I figured I do the thieving, and the rest of you would clear the path, like usual," Kane replied with a shrug.

Malyn produced a small book from the folds of his cloak. "I don't think that's going to work. I found this in the food bag tonight. It wasn't there before."

Kane strained for a better look without leaving her sentry post. The book had a plain cover, a worn leather binding that looked old. In the dim light, she couldn't decipher the lettering on the front. "What's it written in?"

"Renaran, which is an old language used for magic. It fell out of favor a while back, even among academics. You hardly ever see it anymore." He flipped the slim tome back and forth between his fingers. "Which makes me think this is authentic." He raised an eyebrow. "That, and it was slipped into our satchel by a demigoddess."

"Can you read it?"

Malyn nodded. "My schooling was...unconventional. I don't know whether Declan can read Renaran, but I had an elderly tutor who was a stickler for doing things the hard way. He was one of the only reasons I didn't run away sooner."

"So what's it about?"

"It's a history of the Nightshade Monastery, written by a 'Brother Simms.'" Malyn stood and adjusted the shutter on the lantern, then sat on one of the wooden benches built into the wall, still staring out into the cemetery. He raised one leg to rest on the bench, propped the thin book on his thigh, and paged through it, handling the yellowed parchment carefully so it caught the light. "From a quick glance, I'd say he was very interested in its construction—especially its protections."

Kane met his gaze. "So we have the floorplan, and now we have the secrets to how the building is protected?"

Malyn nodded. "Exactly. If you'd like, I'll read it aloud. Maybe between the two of us, we'll figure out what we need to know."

"And stay awake for our watch," Kane added ruefully, with a glance at their sleeping companions. "I'd be lying if I said I wasn't dead tired."

"That's part of the quest, I'm sure," Malyn said, stifling a yawn. "Break us down, strip away our barriers, test our beliefs and our bonds to each other. It's always about more than just retrieving some old trifle, no matter how valuable. I imagine that seer—and maybe some of her god-type friends—can see us, maybe even take bets on whether we make it or not. It's what they do to amuse themselves."

"I imagine if you're immortal, playing cards gets tiresome."

"I hope I never know."

Kane sat on the opposite bench, facing the gate to the road. Within the lychgate's protections, the night outside seemed even darker. She caught glimpses of movement in the shadows, and the song of the forest grew even less harmonious, full of screeches and squeals like dying prey, or the growls and grunts of fighting predators. The outlines of the shadows did not look like any creatures Kane had ever seen or heard tell of. They were the stuff of nightmares. She was relieved for a distraction. One look at Malyn's expression as he regarded the darkened graveyard suggested he felt the same.

"It's not a thick book. I might get it read by the time our watch is over."

"Can you read a little of it in Renaran?"

"Better not. Words have power, and that language was developed for spellcasting. I may not be a mage like Declan, but I'd rather not take the chance."

"Then why write a history book in it?" Kane asked.

"Well, it cuts down on how many people could read it, if the contents were meant to be secret."

"Do you think the book itself is a spell?"

Malyn's brows rose as if he had not considered that possibility. "I don't know. I'll pay attention for that. It would be...unusual." He cleared his throat. "Since I'll have to translate as I read—and I'm a bit rusty—this won't exactly be like listening to an adventure tale."

Last winter, when they had been bored to tears, Kane had stolen a couple of books from the home of one of her marks, both volumes of tales of the gods. Malyn and Declan had read to them to pass the long nights, and they had all found it far more enjoyable than any of them chose to admit.

"It'll be better, because it's real—and we have to live through the adventure. Start reading."

Malyn had a pleasant voice, and the longer he read, the more his voice took on the cultured tones of Trinadon's upper classes, and he lost the twang of Kortufan's streets. Kane wondered if he knew. She kept her eyes on the road beyond the gate but followed along as Malyn recounted the founding of the Order of Nightshade and how the building came to be. Kane wondered what kind of portent it was that the monastery was named for a legendary poison.

"All right, now we're getting to something important," Malyn commented, after skipping over parts of several pages which he assured her were nothing but boring lists of names of people who gave money, or tedious lists of supplies and materials used in the building process.

"This says that the monks brought out the bodies of their dead, which had been laid to rest in caves, and buried them anew in a large circle around the monastery, to serve as a first line of protection."

"So there's your cue," Kane observed. "Get us past the ghosts."

Malyn bent his head to continue reading, only to look up again a few pages later, after recounting the creation of "warriors of clay, who obey only the word of the gods."

"What does that mean?"

Malyn looked up. "There are legends about mages able to fashion life-sized dolls out of mud and clay and enchant them to follow simple orders. Golems, the legends called them. Soulless, basically mindless. Feral. They work without tiring, but they have no intelligence. So if you create one to carry loads from one place to another, that's all they'll ever do. And if the spell isn't crafted right, to be very specific, they'll continue filling a wagon past the point it can hold cargo, until the wheels break, unless their master tells them to pause."

"So these…golems…would make tireless sentries."

"And dangerous ones," Malyn replied. "They might do nothing for decades, but if they've been spelled to protect, and an intruder enters their area—"

"They wake up, and things get bloody," Kane finished for him.

"Yes. I'm afraid so."

Kane glanced at Declan, who seemed to be getting a solid few candlemarks of sleep. "Can he handle them? Is his magic strong enough?"

Malyn thought for a moment, then nodded. "I believe so. Of course, the question is—does *he* believe so?"

"All right, so vengeful ghosts and feral golems and we haven't even gotten in the front door yet. What else?"

Malyn read again, then hesitated. "That's interesting."

"What?"

"The monks must have had some unusual members in their group. The main door can't be unlocked from the outside." He held up a hand to silence Kane's protest. "But there is a small door to one side through which a dog or a similar-sized creature might enter, and then open the door for his companions."

"So they were shifters?"

"Apparently. At least some of them. Or very good dog trainers."

Malyn went back to reading aloud, describing the art and relics in the cloister and their significance, and then skipping again when the book traced the lineage of the monastery's founders.

"Ah...back to something useful," he said finally after a few minutes of flipping pages. "Apparently, the library itself is spelled because it holds dangerous knowledge, rare books, and magical items that should not be handled lightly. In fact, the only one who can use the key Lady Brewer gave us is someone without magic."

"Kieron," Kane said, meeting his gaze.

"In our case, yes. So that also answers the question about the key."

"I thought the key was for the Crypt of the Renounced, where the splinter of the crown is hidden?"

"There's another trial after the library, where we have to get the crypt key, remember? I think that one's going to be my trial."

"So what about the gem?"

Malyn shook his head. "No mention of payment or that there's even anyone around *to* pay. But once we're in the library, I think it's your show."

"What do you mean?" Despite herself, Kane was intrigued.

"Can you read Elvish?"

Kane squirmed, uncomfortable. "Yes. But I haven't in a long time. And there are dialects. Plus, it changed over time, so depending on how old—"

"Yes, yes," Malyn said and made a dismissive gesture. "Good. Because according to this, you'll have to find a hidden elvish box, retrieve it from somewhere awkward, and work the lock correctly the first time."

"Doesn't sound too bad."

"I doubt they'll make it easy, even for someone with your skills," Malyn warned.

"What's in the box?"

Malyn sighed. "I think it's another map, of the Crypt of the Renounced. It's hidden because it's supposedly unholy."

"Cursed?"

"Maybe."

"Fawk. How do we carry it around with us if it's cursed?"

Malyn chuckled. "In its box, of course. Where the monks stored it. Maybe it's lined with lead. Probably engraved with spells."

"If it's cursed, how do we know it won't act against us when we get to the crypt?"

"We don't. If it were easy, they'd have sent a messenger."

Kane drummed her fingers against the wood as a variety of scenarios ran through her mind. She had always prided herself on considering every outcome she could imagine and thinking of how to deal with it. That meant once she was on the ground, in the thick of things, few possibilities were likely to throw her off her game.

"What about getting out again? Does it say anything about traps to keep us in?"

Malyn skimmed the rest of the book, which he said had become bogged down in the rules of the monastic order and academic quibbles. Finally, he looked up. "No. At least, not that they mentioned in here. I'll go through it again. But they didn't seem to be worried that anyone who actually got the map would want to leave with it."

"What about the monks?" Kane asked. "How do we get around them?"

Malyn looks down at the book in his hands. "This is very old. We don't even know if the monastery is still in use. It could be abandoned."

"But all the traps, they'd keep running," Kane said.

"I'd assume so. If the magic was done right."

"Shite." Kane got up and paced. "All right. I figured I'd just go in and lift the map, while the rest of you kept the guards busy or distracted the monks."

"And I know you like to do it your way," Malyn said. "Which works some of the time. But I think the seer sent us because one person can't do all this alone."

"I don't like the way the quest in the monastery is set up," Kane admitted, walking four steps in one direction and then turning to retract her path. "It's like it had us in mind. And yet, it was Kieron's idea to go to the Poxy Dragon. So how—"

"If Lady Leota is really a demigoddess, neither time nor reason work the same for her as they do for us," Malyn replied. "Best not to think on it too hard."

Kane glanced at the notch on the candle in the lantern. Their watch had passed quickly, though there was still a while until dawn.

"Time to wake Kieron and Mitchell. Let Declan sleep. He'll need his magic for the golems," Kane said, making no effort to hide her yawn. She gently shook Kieron's shoulder, while Malyn took a safer route and used a stick to poke Mitchell, keeping himself out of range should his friend wake up swinging.

Both men roused slowly, an indication they had slept well. They stepped over the warded circle, doing their best not to jostle Declan. Kane and Malyn took their place within the rope warding, and immediately Kane felt the extra level of protection envelop them. After the conversation with Malyn, she had expected to be unable to sleep, with her thoughts racing about the dangers and uncertainties ahead. Instead, safe within the circle, Kane fell into a deep, dreamless sleep.

"COME ON. It's time to get on the road." Kieron poked Kane in the shoulder. She and Malyn were the last to rise. Even Declan was up, looking much better than he had since they had left Kortufan. Kane felt too good to gripe about not being awakened sooner and found her good mood to be unusual and a bit unsettling.

"Here." Malyn held out a chunk of bread and cheese for a cold breakfast. Kane ate them quickly, surprised at how hungry she was, and swallowed down some water.

"Did you tell them about the book?"

Malyn nodded. "First thing."

"And?" Kane had somehow thought her companions might be more concerned, knowing what they were going up against.

"Mitchell said it was better than he feared. Kieron agreed. And I think Declan's just happy that you're the one needing to deal with the enchanted box and not him. So overall, they're fine with it."

"Huh." Kane thought there might have been some quibbling over who would do what, but everyone seemed to fall into their appointed roles without concern. That was something else she liked about this small, damaged "family"—they had their faults, but none of them were as prideful as an elf. The elves she had known, and even the half-elves like herself, would have vied for the role that might seem the most prestigious, regardless of whose skill best served the need. Kieron and the others, by comparison, were practical, and no one stood on ceremony.

"Wait." Declan's voice made them pause before they left the protection of the lychgate. "I have an idea." He unrolled the warded rope he had used the night before. "This might be a bit awkward, but I think the extra protection will be worth it. Pass this around," he instructed, handing off one end of the rope to Kieron and holding onto the other, "so it encircles us. If we match our stride, we can stay inside the warding."

"You're kidding, right?" Kieron asked.

Declan shook his head. "No. Did you sleep well last night?"

Kieron nodded. "Better than in a long while."

"We all did," Malyn replied. "The extra warding helped." He pulled the end of the rope out of Kieron's hand. "I'll hold onto the rope, if it's too much of a burden for you."

Kane chuckled at the annoyance on Kieron's face, but they formed a tight group with Kane taking point, then Kieron and Declan, followed by Mitchell and Malyn. The rope was long enough to encircle them without crowding, so long as everyone watched where they walked.

Kane braced herself as they stepped out of the lychgate. The energy shifted, but not as badly as she had feared. The rope's magic buffered the worst of the unpredictable magic beyond the edge of the Corpse Road, easing the discomfort Kane had expected.

Still, the Shadow Woods remained dangerous, and none of them lowered their guard. Kane sensed the twisted magic surging and waning beyond the road's boundaries. Even with all of their protections, she felt as if she was fighting the current as if just walking took more effort than it should.

"Do you feel that?" Declan asked after they had traveled for nearly a candlemark.

"You mean the feeling that we're walking through treacle?" Mitchell responded.

"The forest is fighting us," Malyn replied. "It would be worse without the extra warding."

"How much farther?" Kieron sounded worried. Kane wondered what the human sensed of the unnatural energy around them, since he possessed no magic of his own. Sometimes, she thought that might be an advantage, not to be conscious of the tangle of forces that raged all around. Then again, the lack of magic amounted to a form of blindness, losing the early warning that came with heightened and extended senses. She remained undecided.

"We're nearly out," Kane said. "If we can hold it together a little longer, we'll be safe."

"You mean, we'll be past one danger, and heading into another," Mitchell replied.

Kane shrugged. "I prefer to think that we're another segment closer to going home."

The closer they got to the edge of the Shadow Woods, the stronger the energy currents that buffeted them became, so that even with the additional warding Kane and the others found themselves struggling as if they battled a strong wind. By the time they reached the border, they had linked arms, anchoring each other with their bodies and their magic to overcome the assault.

As they neared the border, Kane felt her anxiousness grow, remembering the close call with the bridge in the Deadlands. She couldn't believe the Shadow Woods would give them up easily.

"Shite," Kane muttered under her breath when they reached the edge of the forest. The others crowded behind her, and she heard them echo her concern with various profanities.

A chasm stretched ahead. Far below, a wide river raged. Spanning the gap was a wooden bridge suspended from ropes.

"Is the bridge spelled?" Kane asked Declan. The mage closed his eyes and went still for a moment, then nodded.

"Yes. Not cursed, but it is enchanted. I suspect it was done to keep anyone from leaving, though whether this side did it to keep people in or the other side wanted to keep anyone from here out, I don't know."

Mitchell edged closer. "Could the spell have a protection aspect? There's no one around to maintain the bridge, but it looks like it's in fairly good shape."

"Maybe. But I don't think that's all of it," Declan warned.

Mitchell took another step onto the first plank of the bridge. He recoiled, jumping back. "I was wrong. Half the boards are missing, and the ropes are frayed. That thing's a deathtrap!"

Kane and the others exchanged glances. The bridge looked the same as it had when Mitchell made his first assessment. Kane ventured closer. "It looks fine from here." She stepped onto the first board and scrambled backward. "Gods and goddess, the whole thing is on fire!"

Declan walked toward the bridge while Kane regained her composure. He stopped just before taking that first step, then after a moment's pause, shifted forward. Like the others, he hastily withdrew. "The bridge is an illusion that doesn't exist, and we would all plunge to our deaths."

Malyn's eyes narrowed, and he edged near. When he took a step onto the bridge, he did not recoil, but every muscle in his body tensed with the effort. After a moment, he moved back, visibly relaxing.

"The bridge is spelled. It's not really on fire, non-existent, falling apart, or as I saw it, leading us into the Dark Abyss. I have a theory. Kieron, what do you see?"

Kieron glanced at the others nervously then approached the bridge as if it were a wild animal, ready to strike. When he reached the first step, he braced himself and moved forward. After a moment, he took a second step, then turned around, standing on the bridge, to face the rest of them. "I see a bridge. It's in decent shape. I'm not sure I understand the problem."

Malyn and Declan exchanged a glance. "Kieron sees the bridge as it is," Malyn said. "Because he's the only one of us without magic. Whoever placed the spell either wanted to keep those with magic out of what lays across the chasm, or hold them within the Shadow Woods."

"What happens if you aren't looking?" Kieron asked.

"You mean if we have our eyes closed?" Kane started to laugh at the notion and stopped. *Could it be that simple?*

"Suppose it's really a spell that plays on your fears," Kieron said. "If you have your eyes shut, it can't show you awful things. You keep your eyes shut, we keep the rope warding around us to dampen the bad magic, and I lead you across."

As if the Shadow Woods knew it was about to lose its intended victims, Kane felt the energy disruption on either side of the Corpse Road flux and flow. "I think we need to do something, because the forest wants us to stay, and if we wait too long, it's going to figure out how to make that happen."

"I'm game." Mitchell moved up to stand behind Kieron. "What do you think? Single file?"

Kieron nodded. "Form a chain, holding hands, and in the other hand, hold onto the spelled rope and loop it down and back. And hope for the best."

To Kane's elven senses, the bent and twisted energies raged like a storm against the protections of the Corpse Road. She did not want to discover what would happen if those forces broke loose.

"Count me in." She linked hands with Mitchell and gave a challenging look to Malyn and Declan. "Well?"

Malyn maneuvered so Declan would be between him and Kane, and brought up the rear. They quickly passed the rope around and back up, so that Kieron held both ends in one hand while holding fast to Mitchell with the other.

"Close your eyes," Kieron ordered. "Here we go. Just keep walking, stay connected, and whatever you do, don't open your eyes."

The bridge Kane had glimpsed was made of boards knotted into thick rope supports, with two side ropes to hold onto, and nothing that would stop someone from plummeting to their death if they fell. She tried very hard not to think of the chasm, the drop, or the raging river beneath them as she took her first step behind Mitchell and braced herself.

Nothing happened. She fought the temptation to feel relieved, remaining wary for some other trap. The bridge swayed with their movement, but her elven agility made that of little consequence. Kane's balance enabled her to move among the high branches of tall trees or run across the roof ridges in the city. If this shakiness was as bad as the bridge passage got, she felt like it was a good deal.

Mitchell's hand clasped hers tightly. She had no idea what he made of the bridge sway, and the slight undulation as Kieron led them from one plank to another. But whatever Mitchell was experiencing had his muscles clenched and his fingers digging into her palm. Behind her, Declan's hand was clammy, damp with sweat, and he groaned in discomfort. She had no contact with Malyn in the back and hoped that he could handle himself because Declan sounded like he was fighting down panic.

"You're all doing fine," Kieron coaxed. The encouraging tone was jarring coming from Kieron, who was more likely to bark at them to get their asses moving than to wheedle or cajole. Kane heard the slightest tremor in his voice, which told her that the situation unnerved him, and that he felt the weight of responsibility for leading his companions safely through the trial.

Kane counted the steps, though she had no idea how many it would take to reach the other side. Perhaps the length of the bridge had been an illusion as well, and now that they were committed, it stretched even farther than they had expected. Maybe that was the truth Kieron knew and dared not share with them.

Everything in Kane urged her to open her eyes, to take control, to manage for herself. But she remembered the surge of panic she had felt when she had tried to cross on her own and knew that succumbing to terror now would likely kill them all, or send at least some of them plunging to the bottom. She bit her lip, tasting blood, and focused on her count, returning the vise-grip on Mitchell's hand and digging the spelled rope into her other palm as touchstones of reality.

With every step, the bridge moved back and forth and up and down as their weight shifted one by one. Kane had navigated much trickier footing jumping between rooftops or walking her way like an acrobat on a rope strung between two posts. A full bridge with solid boards and strong rope should have made her feel secure. Yet even with her eyes shut and her concentration focused, some of the bridge's spell still bled into her mind, making every step a fight.

All at once, the bridge bucked and swung, nearly toppling Kane, making her clutch for the railing while still holding tight to the spelled rope. Had the bridge suddenly been cut loose? Were storm winds gusting down the canyon? She fought instinct and kept her eyes shut, but her jaw clenched tightly enough; she thought she might break a tooth.

"Easy." Kieron had a note of alarm in his voice. "Whatever you think is happening, there's nothing wrong. I'm going to move faster to get us through. Stay together, and we'll make it. We're almost to the other side."

Kane felt the rough side rope burn against her right palm where she and Declan had twined their fingers and gripped it together. The cool of the spelled cord slid between joined hands on her left, where Mitchell's grip was bruisingly tight. Declan's grip had eased, and she didn't know whether that meant he had gotten his fears under control or that he was succumbing to the terrors in his mind and might drop away at any instant.

If he lets go, what then? I don't dare open my eyes to search for him. In response, Kane tightened her grip, and Declan squeezed back in confirmation.

One step after another, over one hundred in all, before they finally stepped off of the bridge and onto solid ground. Kane felt the spell break, and the tightness in her gut eased.

"You can open your eyes now," Kieron said.

The place where they stood looked utterly unremarkable. No dead husks of trees, or twisted magic, no lurking creatures or folded reality, just a clearing, and a road that led toward the horizon. Kane hadn't been so happy to see "nothing" in a long time.

"There's nothing magical here," Declan said, after reading their surroundings.

Malyn nodded. "No restless ghosts or strange energy. As far as I can tell, it's exactly what it looks like—ordinary."

They turned to Mitchell for his appraisal. "I'm not picking up anything odd, either. No scent of predators or dead bodies. Nothing that sets off my wolf. That doesn't mean we're safe," he cautioned. "It just means none of the usual things are trying to kill us."

"Always an optimist," Kane said. She looked at Kieron. "I'm not sensing anything strange, either. The plants and trees seem normal. I think whatever this part of the quest has in store for us, at least the landscape isn't trying to kill us."

"I'll take whatever breaks we get," Kieron replied. He rolled up the spelled rope and handed it back to Declan, who returned it to his bag.

Kane glanced at the bridge. From this side, it did look quite ordinary. A single road led away from the bridge, and a glance at the map showed that it would soon branch and cross over other roads on the way to the monastery. A few small towns dotted their path.

"It's still early," she said. We should be able to reach the monastery by afternoon. Maybe we can get what we came for and be on our way." Kane doubted it would be so simple, and her jaunty words projected a confidence she did not really feel.

"There's another lychgate, not far beyond the monastery," Kieron noted after glancing at the map. "If all goes well, we can make that by nightfall." What he didn't say but that Kane and the others knew was that the timing all depended on whether their efforts at the monastery succeeded.

The stretch of road between the bridge and the first crossroad was deserted. But once they passed the crossroad, other travelers shared the road, exchanging polite nods and reserved acknowledgments. After days of being alone in the Deadlands and Shadow Woods, Kane found that the presence of strangers made her twitchy.

"Relax," Mitchell said, walking beside her. "They don't know why we're here, and they don't care."

"I care. I feel...exposed."

"How is it different from every road leading out of Kortufan, which we've traveled more times than I can count?" Mitchell replied.

Kane shrugged, feeling out of sorts. "It just is. Maybe because we belong there. This," she said with a wave of her hand to indicate their surroundings, "isn't our place."

"We'll be gone soon enough, I hope," Mitchell said. "Let's see if we can make quick work of the monastery."

Late in the morning they passed a weathered-looking pub. From the number of horses tethered to the hitching posts outside, it looked to be doing a brisk business. Kieron paused outside, and they regarded the tavern for a moment. "Do we go in?" he asked.

Kane shuddered as she recalled Lady Brewer's inn. "Bad idea," she warned. "We don't need the food, we don't want the locals paying attention to us, and we already have the map and information we need for the next part of the quest. It can only cause trouble."

Mitchell nodded. "I agree. Anything we could learn about them is canceled out by having them learn something about us."

"Too many strangers," Declan replied.

"Nothing to gain, plenty to lose. We can stop for ale at the Poxy Dragon, after we collect our winnings," Malyn put in.

They hefted their bags and kept walking. This stretch of the road passed through open land, with meadows and farm fields. In the distance, Kane saw barns and houses. Sheep, cows, and goats grazed behind neat fences. Their surroundings looked utterly ordinary, and Kane found that suspicious and disturbing.

"I don't trust this," she murmured to Mitchell.

"The map?"

Kane shook her head. "No. This place. I feel like it's trying to lull us into a false sense of security."

Mitchell stared at her as if she'd turned green. "Seriously? It looks just like back home, once you've gotten outside the city."

"That's what I mean."

"Kane, the seer sent us to a real place. This is someone's home. I'm finding it encouraging that there are people living here, going about their business."

"I don't like people in general. Strangers are worse."

Mitchell chuckled. "You're more elf-ish than usual today. Next, you'll be telling us the food and wine aren't up to your standards."

Kane made a rude gesture, and Mitchell laughed. "I just don't want to get taken by surprise," she replied.

"Understandable—but I'm still going to take the chance we've got to breathe a little easier while we can. We'll be back in the thick of things as soon as we reach the monastery," Mitchell said.

Normally, thinking about doing a job gave Kane a buzz of excitement. But infiltrating the monastery filled her with dread. She tried to clear her mind and focus on the satisfaction of pulling off a successful job, and the intrigue of the puzzle itself. Instead, she had a knot in her stomach. Kane resolved to keep her senses sharp.

"There it is," Kieron said as they came to a rise in the road. Nightshade Monastery was a box-like stone building three stories tall with a slate roof and a high wall around it. From their vantage on the hill, they could see into the compound. No one moved about between the main building and the smaller dependencies, and no smoke rose from the chimney. Nearby fields that might once have been tended by the monks lay fallow and forgotten, and no livestock grazed in the pastures.

"Looks abandoned," Mitchell remarked.

Malyn and Declan moved closer, making their own assessment. "Definitely haunted," Malyn replied after a moment. "Lots of restless spirits all around the outside of the wall. They're strong enough that I can't tell whether there are more inside the building."

"Plenty of magic, too," Declan said. "Enough to animate those golems the book described."

"But we know how to get around those problems, right?" Kieron confirmed. "So once Mitchell gets us inside, Kane and I just need to collect the goods."

"Did you forget the part about the box being cursed?" Malyn asked.

"I was hoping that turned out to be a misunderstanding," Kieron answered.

"Let's get this over with." Kane's clipped tone cut through their banter.

No one attempted to stop them as they approached the compound. The dirt road that veered off from the main highway was overgrown, another sign of disuse. As they drew closer, they saw the high weeds and broken pasture fences that suggested abandonment.

"I wonder what made them leave?" Kieron mused.

"Maybe the order died out," Malyn replied. "It happens. A sect springs up, gains followers, and then it loses popularity over time. We don't even know to which god the monks were dedicated, or whether they were scholars instead."

A dry gully separated the road from the monastery grounds. The arched stone bridge that crossed the gully looked solid. Yet Kane felt a gut-deep hesitation to cross. On the other side, cairns and mounds dotted the ground. Farther away, large brown boulders had been placed at intervals around the stone wall that surrounded the monastery building.

"They really didn't want to be disturbed," Kieron joked.

"Or they were charged with safeguarding objects that shouldn't get out," Declan suggested.

Mitchell looked at the mage. "You think there might be other cursed or dangerous relics in there, besides the box?"

Declan shrugged. "It wouldn't surprise me. There are brotherhoods of mages who don't take vows in service to any particular god. They aren't overly religious. Their point in forming the community is to protect and preserve knowledge and artifacts. To keep it from being lost, or from getting into the wrong hands. With the kind of protections around Nightshade, and the fact that it's named for a deadly flower, I suspect they were the knowledge guardian type. And don't forget the witch's warning to take only the box."

That made Kane even less happy, but she said nothing.

"Why would the map be in a cursed box?" Mitchell asked.

"Maybe whoever put it there didn't want to destroy the map, but they didn't want anyone to get it, either," Kieron said.

"So how are we supposed to get the map out of the box if it's cursed?" Kane asked. That question had bothered her since Malyn had read through the book.

"I think there's a code in the book," Malyn replied. They all looked at him, as this was news he hadn't bothered to share. He shrugged. "I didn't want to say anything until I'd worked it out. But I've been thinking on it as we traveled, and I'm pretty sure I know how to use the code to find the counter spell that's hidden in the book."

"Pretty sure?" Kane echoed.

"By the time we need it, I'll have it," Malyn said confidently.

"How do we get a cursed box out of the monastery without getting...cursed ourselves?" Kane asked.

Declan withdrew the warded rope and reinforced its protections. "Here," he said, handing her the rope. He had woven part of the rope into a loose pouch. "As soon as you find the box, wrap the rope all around it. That should contain the magic until Malyn can work the counter spell to get rid of the curse. Then Kane can decipher the elvish and tell Kieron how to unlock it."

Kane took the cord and slung the coil over her shoulder like a climbing rope. "You have the key and the floorplan?" she asked Kieron.

He produced both, showing the key on a chain around his neck, and the floorplan safe in a pouch at his waist. "At your service, m'lady." Kieron grinned, giving an exaggerated bow.

Kane surveyed the distance to the wall. "How's this going to work?"

"I'll go first," Malyn said. "I'll handle the ghosts and make a safe corridor for the rest of you to pass over."

"I'll deal with the golems," Declan added. "All you need to worry about is getting to the gate."

"I guess that's where I come in," Mitchell said. "I think I'm just going to go wolf the whole time, unless I need to shift back on the other side to work the door. I'll get you in, and then wait for you in the courtyard." Mitchell moved several yards away and stripped down, putting his clothing in his pack which he stashed at the side of the stone bridge. Kane and the others had seen him shift before, but it was not pleasant to hear his cries of pain or the sounds of breaking bones and rending flesh.

Kane watched for threats as Mitchell shifted to his wolf. She and Kieron left their bags with Mitchell's, carrying only essentials. Mitchell, now in wolf form padded up beside Kane and gave her hand a lick with his long tongue, amusement sparkling in his yellow eyes. She made a noise and wiped her hand on her pants, while Mitchell trotted off, looking satisfied.

"I guess that covers it," Kane said, still antsy. "Let's go. The sooner we're done, the sooner we can get out of here."

Malyn moved to the front of the group, with the others walking two abreast behind him. As soon as they crossed over the stone bridge, the temperature dropped enough for them to see their breath. Wisps of fog and green foxfire rose from the cairns and mounds, shrieking and keening.

"I've got this," Malyn said quietly, and then opened up his power.

The ghosts flocked toward him, forming a glowing, pulsating cloud. Malyn closed his eyes, and Kane felt the energy around them shift. Malyn's magic flared, pulling the ghosts closer, as Kane and the others sprinted past in the safe space he had opened for them.

She dared a glance behind once they reached the other side. Malyn was barely visible inside a roiling mist. She hoped he had not volunteered for more than he could handle.

"My turn," Declan said. They had no sooner passed the last cairn and stepped onto the wide stone walkway that ran around the wall before one of the large rock "balls" uncurled. The golem had the form of a man, but the clay face was featureless, and the body completely smooth. It looked like a mud doll, until the creature began to move.

The golem swung at Declan, who dodged out of its way. The fist slammed into the rock wall with enough force to break off some of the stone, sending down a rain of rock dust. The strike was clearly meant to kill.

Each footfall shook the ground as the golem moved for another blow. On either side, more golems woke from their slumber. Kane could see the gate. But as more of the giants lumbered toward them, she wasn't sure how they could reach it.

"I'm going to draw their attention and place a distraction spell on you," Declan called over his shoulder, unconcerned if the golems could hear him. "Count to five, then run really fast for the gate. I'll hold the spell as long as I can, but I might get busy." Just then, the golem swung once more, and while Declan danced out of the way, Kane knew it would become more difficult to avoid the blows as more golems joined the fight.

"Go!" Declan shouted.

Kane, Kieron, and Mitchell sprinted for the gate. Mitchell reached it first, since in his wolf form he was the fastest. Just as the book had described, an opening too short and narrow for most men but sized right for a large dog was next to the big wooden gates. Mitchell gave a yip, then belly-crawled through the passage.

Kane looked back toward where they'd started. Declan was ringed by four of the golems, holding his own as magic flared from his hands, knocking the creatures back or sending them stumbling. The sea of ghosts around Malyn seemed to have thinned, and Kane wondered if the monastery's designers had given thought to having a true medium attempt to skirt their protections.

The creak and groan of the huge gate moving on its hinges brought her attention back. Mitchell didn't try to open the door fully, just enough for Kane and Kieron to slip inside. He gave another yip, then sat next to the opening mechanism and bid them hurry with a dip of his head.

Kane and Kieron had studied the floorplan on their journey. Kane was used to navigating a mark's house blind, so knowing where they were going was a gift. Kieron hid his nervousness well, but Kane could tell he worried about what they might find inside.

If the monastery had any living residents, surely they would know by now that their security had been breached. Kane heard the shrieking ghosts and the thump and bang of the golems echoing in the bailey as she and Mitchell raced for the main building. The square monastery was simple, but built of beautifully laid stone, with mullioned windows and a vaulted roof. Perhaps the monks were contemplative, in addition to whatever their devotion or discipline. Whatever they were, none seemed to be in residence, since no one sounded an alarm or rushed out to intercept them.

The front door was unlocked.

They walked into an entranceway that ran from front to back, with two rooms opening off to either side and a stairway rising to the second floor. According to the floorplan, the library was on the third, so if the building had any remaining occupants or hidden traps, they were likely to find out above.

Kane led the way, counting on her elven agility and heightened senses to alert her to danger. Kieron watched behind them to make sure there were no unpleasant surprises sneaking up from the rear. The second floor held rows of doorways into what Kane assumed were the monks' bedchambers. Another flight of stairs brought them to the third floor, which had two doorways on the right side of the hallway, but only one on the left.

"I've got the key ready," Kieron said, moving past Kane. He pulled the key Lady Brewer had given them and stopped to get a better look at the heavy oaken door. The fine wood was carved with runes and sigils from top to bottom, and the ironwork that held it to its hinges was also worked with intricate magical marks. "I'll wait by the door unless you need me."

He turned the key in the lock. The old mechanism clicked then clunked as the tumblers worked. Kieron turned the knob, and the door swung open.

Kane wasn't a mage, and her elven senses were strongest in nature, but the reek of dark magic made her recoil when the warded door opened.

"What's wrong?" Kieron asked.

Kane waved him away. "Stay back. There's just...a lot of bad stuff in there."

The large room looked like a cross between a library and a museum. Wooden built-in shelves covered the walls from floor to the very high ceiling. They held a mix of books, manuscripts, and objects. In the center of the floor, freestanding bookcases and shelves stood in rows. Kane's heart sank at the idea of needing to search for the box amid all the many thousand objects.

She stepped farther into the room and saw a keyhole built into the wooden paneling beside the door. "See if your key fits there," she directed Kieron, who did as she requested.

Kieron turned the key in the new lock, and a series of flat planks slid out from between the shelves on the wall, forming an ascending cantilevered staircase that led to a glass-enclosed shelf at the very top corner of the room.

"Give me the key," Kane said, eyeing the rise between the steps as the idea hit her.

"But it won't work for you," Kieron objected.

"Trust me." There was no rail, and a fall from the upper end would be bad, but the climb was nothing compared to the heights she had scaled in the city or in the high trees. Her elven agility would get her up—and hopefully down. But her gut told her that retrieving the item would not be as easy as it appeared.

Kieron handed Kane the key, and she wrapped the strap around her wrist, securing the key snuggly against her skin. With the warded rope still coiled over her shoulder, Kane tested the first step. It held her weight without sinking, so she took the next step, expecting the support to suddenly vanish. She carefully made her way from step to step, leery of touching the shelves on the left side without knowing their contents.

Dark magic fouled the room's resonance, seeming to come from everywhere at once. No one source stood out like a beacon; instead, the sense of rot and discord came from hundreds—maybe thousands—of points throughout the room. Some of those points came from the glass cabinet at the top of the cantilevered steps, and Kane knew that the box she sought was one of them.

They had seen no one in the monastery, but now Kane felt watched —and judged. The room took note of her, or rather, the powerful objects in the room did. Some of them bordered on sentient.

Come this way.

I can make you rich.

All your dreams can come true.

I can give you vengeance—or love.

Make you so powerful, no one can hurt you again.

The voices whispered to her, growing louder as she climbed. She dared not glance back at Kieron for fear of losing her balance, but she wondered if the human was deaf to the entreaties, or merely perceived the room as "unsettling."

The closer to the cabinet Kane got, the more her thoughts turned to the betrayal she had experienced from her people, and her grief for her parents and what she lost. Anger warred with loss. The voices grew louder and something in their tone sounded satisfied.

Abruptly, Kane wrested control of her thoughts back from where they had strayed. *I will not be used,* she snarled silently to the forces that vied for her attention.

She quickened her pace, less afraid of a misstep than she was of being ensnared by the promises and lies held out to her by objects eager to end their banishment and captivity. At the top, she confronted the glass-enclosed shelf. Inside, more than a dozen arcane relics sat carefully spaced. There were several boxes, but thanks to the book that Malyn found in their bag, she knew what to look for. It sat in the center, unremarkable except for the elvish runes carved into the wood, a small octagonal black box.

Carved into the frame of the door and etched onto the glass itself was a phrase in what Kane recognized as Old Elvish. She struggled to translate, but the meaning, when it became clear, chilled her. *"Think. All actions have consequences. Have you weighed the cost?"*

"Shite," Kane muttered. The key's strap was securely wrapped around her wrist so there was no chance of dropping it. The voices and taunts grew to a crescendo.

Kane opened the door, readying the spelled rope and a pouch Malyn had found in the pack the seer had given them. She extended the hand holding the key, and as soon as she got near the box, Kane realized that the library's voices had gone silent. The box drew the key on her wrist like a magnet.

It felt as if the room held its breath.

Making sure to only touch the box with the spelled rope, she tipped it into the pouch and then secured the pouch with the rope. The step beneath her began to withdraw into the wall.

"Kane!" Kieron yelled in warning.

Falling to the floor beneath wasn't an option. She'd surely break a bone, or worse. But Kane had a lifetime's experience of staying aloft in the moving branches of a forest and on rickety ledges and drainpipes in the city. She pushed off while she still had some of the step left beneath her, and caught hold with her hands and feet on two shelves in the adjacent bookcase. The spelled box hung in its rope pouch as Kane dangled from her precarious perch.

She felt the wood begin to give way, as if the whole case might tear loose from the wall. Kane was still too high to fall, so she jumped again, landing this time on one of the large units in the center of the room.

The huge bookshelves wobbled with her weight, and Kane realized that the library itself was attempting to stop a thief, hoping to toss her off onto the hard floor. There was no way that she weighed enough to cause the heavy case to sway, unless it was part of the library's plan to guard against intruders or to prevent the removal of an object consigned for the permanent collection.

"If that case falls, you'll get crushed," Kieron shouted. "Jump. I'll catch you."

Kane was still too high to fall without getting hurt. Yet the thought of depending on someone to catch her made her hesitate, unwilling to trust. But as the heavy case began to rock back and forth, Kane knew she had to leap or risk being turned to pulp beneath the shelving. No other landing place she could reach would be any more stable, and she did not relish the idea of breaking bones.

"Jump now, Kane!"

Kane pushed off, hoping her kick set the wobbling bookcase back on steady feet. She leaped into the air and fell.

She landed hard in Kieron's arms, with enough momentum to send him to his knees. But he did not drop her, although they both let out an *oof* as the impact punched the breath from them. Kane hurriedly disentangled herself and dusted off, as Kieron climbed to his feet.

"We need to get out of here," Kieron said. "Even without magic, I think this place is going to mutiny."

The library felt darker than when they arrived, and it seemed to have closed in around them. Kane felt the weight of the box out of proportion to its size and swore it strained against the warded rope.

"Move!" she said, as they sprinted for the door.

The door started to swing shut on its own accord, and Kane realized there was no keyhole on this side. She wedged her body between the door and the frame as Kieron added his strength to keep it open.

"Crawl over me," she said. "If I move, it slams shut, and you'll be stuck."

It required an awkward tangle of arms and legs, and Kane nearly hit Kieron in the eye with an elbow, but he managed to scramble over her, then lean against the door to buy her enough space to wriggle free. Kane quickly unwrapped the key from her wrist and had Kieron lock the door behind them, just in case it might buy them precious extra moments.

"You think that maybe getting that damned splinter back isn't a good idea?" Kieron asked as they ran for the stairs.

"Obviously, somebody thinks that. They went to a lot of trouble to hide the damn thing."

She and Kieron fairly flew down the steps, afraid to see if anything was chasing them. It felt as if the monastery was shrugging off a long sleep to take note of intruders. The temperature plummeted, and Kane was sure that the ghosts of the dead monks were gathering. She doubled her speed, and Kieron kept pace, making for the dog gate where Mitchell sat waiting.

"Run!" Kane yelled to Mitchell. She and Kieron plowed through the thin opening between the heavy outer doors. Mitchell, still in his wolf form, tripped the lever to shut the doors the rest of the way, then shot through the smaller gate as if his tail were on fire.

Declan sent up an explosion with a fiery blast to buy them precious seconds from the golems and joined in behind them as they crossed over to where Malyn held off the swarming ghosts.

"I'll join you at the bridge," Malyn shouted. "Keep going."

Kane and the others hurtled past. But as Kane neared the bridge, she realized Malyn was not behind them.

"Malyn!" she shouted, urging him to disengage and run.

She turned and saw Malyn struggling to hold a churning mass of souls at bay. They roiled like billowing smoke, with faces appearing and vanishing. Malyn's features looked drawn, and his voice sounded hoarse as he chanted.

"We've got to get him," she said to Declan, reversing her course. Kieron had no skills to help, and with Mitchell in wolf form, options were limited.

Kane sprinted back for the healer, with no idea of how she would wrest him free from the spirits if he could not. When she got closer, she saw the toll that holding off the ghosts had taken. Malyn's shook with the effort, and he looked utterly spent. His white-blond hair had escaped from its thick braid, and strands stuck out all over, like a nimbus around his face. Always pale, he looked nearly translucent, as if the magic had made him somewhat less solid.

"You grab him. I'll...do something," Declan said.

Malyn tried to wave them off, but Kane ignored him. "This is a rescue. You don't get a vote." She retrieved the warded rope and looped it up and over Malyn, keeping hold of the pouch that held the spelled box. Contact with the rope seemed to revive him, because Malyn stood straighter and his voice grew louder.

"Come on!" Kane shouted, grabbing the medium by one arm. Malyn protested, but the conflict had exhausted him, and he stumbled toward her when she pulled him off balance.

"Don't look!" Declan warned. He jumped between Malyn and the cloud of spirits and shouted a word of power. A bright flash of light flared, strong enough that even with her eyes averted Kane's vision went red. She didn't wait for her sight to clear. Instead, she dragged Malyn as fast as she could, and he nearly lost his footing trying to keep up.

"Cross over!" Declan shouted. The others did not hesitate. Mitchell outpaced them all. Kieron grabbed his bag and Mitchell's and followed. Kane plucked her bag and the one that belonged to Malyn from their stash and hit the bridge at a run, as Malyn struggled to keep up. Declan hadn't left his bag at the bridge, and that few seconds saved put him over the threshold of the monastery's protections before the ghosts had recovered from whatever magic he had sent at them.

They did not stop running until they were all too winded to continue. By then, Malyn wheezed in great lungfuls of air and looked like he might pass out. Declan insisted on remaining in the rear, in case any of the spirits could pass the bridge or enlist the ghosts on the other side.

Kieron and Kane exchanged glances. Both were out of breath, but functioning. Mitchell alone seemed unfazed, but his wolf form offered greater speed than his human body. He shifted back and hurriedly dressed, and Kane took perverse joy in the fact that Mitchell's hair was plastered to his head with sweat, meaning that the run had taxed him, at least a little.

"Are you all right?" Kane asked.

Malyn nodded. "Just tired. I helped the ghosts pass over who wanted to, but there were so many, and some of them had become vengeful. Revenants more than regular ghosts." He gave a bitter chuckle. "Probably what the monks intended when they moved the bodies, but unfair to the dead who didn't have a say."

"What do you need?" Kieron fell into step on the other side of Malyn.

"Food. Water. And as long a sleep as I can steal," Malyn replied. "I dare say the next trial is mine." He sounded like he could fall asleep on his feet.

"The lychgate is just ahead," Kieron said. "We'll make an early night of it. I think we could all use the chance to recuperate."

"We've got the event at the Villa of the Commissar tomorrow night," Malyn said, still sounding out of breath. "I need to be ready. It's our best shot—maybe our only chance—to steal the key for the crypt."

"You'll be ready," Kane assured him. "We all will be."

8

TOM AT THE POXY DRAGON

"I ain't had anyone to bury in more than a fortnight," Thaddeus complained. His shovel Bessie rested against the bar next to him, like an old friend. The gravedigger wrapped his dirt-streaked, gnarled fingers around his cup of whiskey. "It's not good to be idle like that." He tossed off the shot and slid his cup across the sticky bar for more.

"I'm about ready to go thump some poor bloke on the head just to give you something to do," Gunnar grumbled. "It's supposed to be a good thing when no one dies."

"It's not like I want it to be someone I know," Thaddeus argued. "It could be a complete stranger. I'd be fine with that. Maybe a merchant on his way past, has a bit of a bad heart, you know? Or someone eats a piece of spoiled meat."

"None of that!" Elsie snapped and gave Thaddeus a whack on the side of the head with her mixing spoon. "Don't you be giving my cooking a bad name!"

No one said a word, never quite sure what would set her off, and it wasn't worth the risk. No one doubted her food tasted better than any other pub's in a day's ride; it was the ingredients she used that caused their stomachs to turn. Knowing Elsie kept the local rat catchers in business was prime fodder for bad dreams.

Maybe that's not entirely fair, Tom amended silently. Most people ate Elsie's cooking and went on to live happy lives—as long as they never learned what was in the stew.

Still, even questionable rumors didn't seem to stop any of the regulars from bellying up to the bar and ordering a meal. And if they got drunk enough, they'd wind up talking about those rumors. Tom didn't care, so long as they made it to the latrine outside if they decided to return the goods, so to speak.

"I'm just sayin'," Thaddeus went on. "I mean, a man's got needs. I don't ask much from life. Diggin' in the dirt, laying some poor sot to rest. It's a simple life I've got, with simple pleasures, but I've got a right to that, ain't I?"

"Thad, we're all with you, mate. But none of us is gonna up and die just so you can plant us with the posies," Gunnar explained. He slid his own drink over in front of Thaddeus. "Now drink yer drink."

Tom replaced Gunnar's drink with a nod of thanks. The only thing worse than when Thaddeus got like this was on those awful nights when Benny the bard left off singing and got drunk enough to expound on philosophy. Although, on second thought, he rambled on so that anyone who didn't want to go home straightaway drank more, so as not to be bothered by his palavering. The trick, Tom knew, was to have a bit of soft wax to fill the ears. Made it harder to hear when the customers shouted at him, but on the whole, that wasn't a bad thing, either.

Benny was in his usual corner in the back, singing a favorite ballad, *My Lady's Eyes.* It was, at least, a favorite of Benny's, and if it were up to him, the bard would sing it nightly. But since the tragic tale of love and loss went on for fifty verses, each more maudlin than the last, Tom had finally put his foot down and insisted on it being performed only every other night. Benny had moped, sobbed, and dramatically threatened to "end it all," but ultimately agreed.

That annoyed some of the patrons, who had placed wagers on the likelihood of the bard's demise.

"When's that last bunch of heroes supposed to come back?" Gunnar asked, contemplating his drink as if it might disclose the secrets of the universe.

"If they come back." Thaddeus sighed like he had uncovered another cosmic conspiracy to rob him of his livelihood.

"Lady Leota didn't say," Tom replied, wiping up the bar. "And I'm not of a mind to ask her. She's been preoccupied of late."

"Seeing into another realm, no doubt," Lucas supplied from his end of the bar. He brought back the empty tankards he had collected in the common room.

"No doubt," Tom agreed drily. He had complete faith that Lady Leota's powers were real. He also suspected that she amused herself by using the trappings of seers to captivate the crowd at the pub she had chosen as her own. Tom figured that Lady Leota and her "heroes' portal" was good for business, and he wasn't fool enough to try to tell a demigoddess what to do.

"Do you want to hear the poem I've been writing?" Lucas asked hopefully.

Gunnar grunted and downed his whiskey in one shot.

Tom smiled at the boy. "Why don't you save it until it's finished? Then you can surprise all of us."

Lucas gave him a grateful nod, and Tom jotted a note to brew up some extra potent whiskey, for when that day finally came.

"I'm bored." Constance sauntered to the bar. "It's been a bad night for betting. No one's gotten in a fight in hours."

"See what I mean?" Thaddeus said, raising his head from his mire of grief. "It's like everything's coming to an end."

Constance regarded the gravedigger with a grimace. "Actually, I was thinking more along the lines of cribbing a card from one of the men playing poker so they'd accuse each other of cheating. You know, get things moving. Been a slow night."

Constance had a repertoire of sleight of hand tricks designed to "liven up" the evening. Most of the regulars were on to her tricks and paid high tips to avoid being on the receiving end. Those tips, along with her cut of the house bets, went a long way to augment the poor wage Tom could afford to pay her.

"Go ahead, but mind that you wait until Benny's done with his song, or we'll never hear the end of it," Tom warned.

Constance rolled her eyes. "You mean, we'll never hear the end of that bloody song. I've had three customers beg me to stab them, and I think only one was joking."

"Huh. Usually they just want you to clap them on the ears and deafen them for an hour or two." Tom poured a round of drinks for the regulars at the bar.

"They know Benny's working up to his big finish," Constance replied, accepting the drink Tom poured for her. She downed it in one slug without batting an eye, something even seasoned sailors often couldn't do with Tom's potent poteen.

"I do wonder about those blokes who went through the wall the last time," Tom said, leaning against the backbar. "I rather liked them. Wonder if they'll make it back?"

"Long odds are on all of them coming home without losing a finger or a limb," Constance replied, scanning the crowd with a bored expression to check for—and simultaneously discourage—anyone wanting a refill. "Two to one odds that the half-elf kills one of her own party. She looked like the type," Constance added when Tom raised an eyebrow.

"And the rest?"

She shrugged. "The smart money is on the pretty blond. A lot of the bets went against him because he's so...refined." Constance leaned in and dropped her voice. "But I think he's probably a hellcat. Definitely more than he appears." She touched a finger to her nose. "I know about these things."

With that, Constance sashayed out into the common room with a full pitcher of beer, not hesitating to twist an ear and flick a nose if someone was slow to pay or tried to pass off the wrong amount. Even the most stout-hearted knew better than to get on her bad side. Thaddeus had a few unmarked graves in the back to attest to what could happen. Tom sighed, taking in how hopeful Thaddeus looked when one of the big lugs who was new to the place looked like he might flirt. A fork in the back of the hand shut that down quickly, much to the amusement of the lug's companions and Thaddeus's bitter disappointment.

Tom moved from behind the bar to bring a drink to Lady Leota, poured from a special bottle she gave him that he kept behind the counter, one which never ran dry. The green liquor sparkled with an inner light, flecked with gold.

"How are they doing?" he asked quietly when he delivered the drink.

Lady Leota took the goblet with a nod of thanks. "They've made good progress," she replied. "Better than most. I am impressed."

"You think they'll be back soon? I've got customers who are antsy about their wagers."

She gave him one of her unreadable smiles. "Your patrons should learn patience. Many paths are still open to the adventurers, and even I cannot see which ones they will choose. Every choice changes the outcome. And the hardest tasks are yet to come."

"That other kingdom waiting for its piece of the crown—that's all real?" Tom sometimes wondered if the quests were a reason unto themselves, stories devised by Lady Leota to justify a dangerous quest.

"Oh yes. Very. Sorenden's fate as a kingdom rests on the actions of these heroes," Lady Leota replied, taking a sip of her drink and savoring the taste. "So I do hope, for all our sakes, that they survive. I'll be very disappointed if they don't. And Sorenden...well, it doesn't bear thinking about what befalls them if the heroes don't return victorious."

"You can't just help them along?" Tom had asked variations of that question many times, but the answer was always the same.

"I've given them all the help I may," she replied. "What happens now is entirely up to them."

9

MALYN

MALYN DIDN'T WANT THE OTHERS TO KNOW HOW MUCH THE FIGHT AT Nightshade had cost him. The ghosts were old and vengeful, and while some longed to cross over, more were eager to take their revenge on the living. Many times he wished that he could use his healing powers on himself.

The monks who dug up and moved the bodies had been thorough. There had been hundreds of ghosts, powerful enough to be dangerous. Even with Malyn's training, keeping the ghosts at bay had been a challenge, badly tiring him. For someone who wasn't a medium, the attempt to cross the cemetery would likely have been fatal.

He did not want to be a burden to his companions, so Malyn did his best to hide how the battle had drained him. Their worried glances told him that he had not fooled anyone, but at least they kept their concerned comments to a minimum.

Thankfully, the lychgate wasn't far. He dreaded contact from the ghosts in the graveyard adjacent to the gate, but to his relief the spirits remained quiet. He reminded himself that the vast majority of ghosts went to their eternal rest without fuss, or hung about in the world of the living for their own purposes without causing trouble. He felt grateful, because the dead were far too numerous for the scant number of mediums.

Still, Malyn sent the residents of the gate graveyard a blessing, assuring them that he and his friends meant no harm. As soon as he stepped under the lychgate, he felt the tension of the day ease.

"You need to sit before you fall down," Declan said. He helped Malyn shrug out of his pack as the others got settled. "Let me have a look at you." Declan wasn't a healer like Malyn, but his magic could do a lot in a pinch.

"I'm not wounded, just exhausted," Malyn told him, trying not to sound ill-humored when he knew his friend was trying to help. Still, all he wanted was some food and water and the chance for a long, unbroken sleep.

"Not all wounds show," Declan replied, insisting on letting his hands hover just above Malyn's form, scanning with his magic.

"How often did the ghosts touch you?" he asked, sitting back on his haunches.

Malyn's cheeks reddened at being caught out. "They were all around me. Some of them got through my shielding."

Declan nodded. "You're not just tired; they've depleted your core."

"What's that?" Kieron asked. "And how bad is it?"

Malyn glared at Declan, although there was no way the five of them could be in such tight quarters and hold a private conversation.

"Core, life energy, soul—it goes by many names. Between the energy it took for him to keep the revenants from pursuing the rest of you and what they were able to leech from him when they got through his barriers, he's badly drained. He needs time to replenish his power."

"How much time?" Mitchell asked. Back in human form, he also showed the effort and strain it had taken to shift.

"I can rest fully when we're safely home," Malyn objected before Declan could say more. "Just feed me and give me enough wine to make me sleep, and I'll be much improved in the morning."

He didn't want his friends to worry, and Declan was known to be a little too detailed and precise when evasion was required. They were all working under pressure, and Malyn didn't want to be coddled. The weight of the quest would be on him once they came to the Villa of the Commissar. He fully intended to be in shape to handle it or to at least bluff his way through.

Declan gave him a look that suggested he knew what Malyn was up to, but didn't press. Mitchell dug into the food pack, withdrawing rations for all of them.

"There are some new things that weren't here before," he noted, pulling out two folded pieces of parchment, each fastened with an embossed wax seal. "There are also two bundles wrapped with paper and twine—they feel like clothing."

"That should get us into the villa, while the rest of you skulk around and create a diversion," Malyn said. He sat on the bench on one side of the lychgate and leaned back against the support post as he ate.

"I don't 'skulk,'" Mitchell said with a sidelong glance and a twitch of his lips. "Curs skulk. Wolves go wherever they damn well please."

"Just don't lift your leg on the guard this time. That was embarrassing," Kane remarked.

Mitchell grinned. "He didn't know what to be more upset about—having a wolf that close, or getting peed on. And don't complain—it worked. I had to improvise."

"I've got some ideas for diversions we can discuss later," Declan said. "But first, let's break the spell on that box Kane and Kieron retrieved."

Tired as he was, Malyn couldn't overcome his curiosity and he sat up, leaning forward to see as Declan took the box out of the pouch and placed it in the center of the lychgate floor, and coiled the spelled rope around it. The mage held one hand palm-down just above the pouch, and closed his eyes, listening to the magic.

"It's not really cursed," Declan said when he finally opened his eyes. "But it is spelled. Good thing Kane had the key on her. That likely kept the spell from fully triggering."

Kane rounded on him. "Are you kidding me? It almost killed me—and it didn't 'fully' trigger the spell?"

Declan shrugged, used to Kane's temper. "It's attuned to the key.

Perhaps there was something else that originally was supposed to be with it. Be glad it blunted the magic—the spellwork is good."

"Can you break it?" Kieron asked, keeping a respectful distance.

"Yes. It's quality work, but not complicated." He frowned for a moment, then dug the book Malyn had found out of the bag. "Hand me the key," Declan said to Kane. "And the gem." Kieron complied. Declan brought the key, gem, and book together with the box, which was still wrapped in the warded rope. The four items flared with green light, then went dark.

"Seems like they're of a set," Declan murmured. "The spell broke on its own, once the other items were nearby."

"Seriously? You mean if I'd had those other poxy things on me when we went into the monastery, the whole bloody building wouldn't have tried to kill us?" Kane looked truly annoyed.

"It's not as if we got the full instructions," Declan replied, miffed at her tone. "But Malyn did work out the code and the counter spell." He unwound the rope and renewed its wardings, then spread the rope in a large circle around them, as he had done before. Once again, Malyn felt the noise of the outside world recede, soothing his frayed nerves. Declan spoke the words of the counter spell, and the box glowed blue, then the light winked out.

"That should take care of the curse," Declan said, though he still watched the box mistrustfully. "Kane, would you translate the runes?"

Malyn watched as Kane knelt next to the box and listened intently as she translated the elvish runes which provided instructions on how to open the box.

"Kieron, if you would do the honors?" Declan held up the key and nodded to the box. "If you forget the steps, stop and Kane will repeat them for you."

Kieron accepted the key and knelt, his hand shaking as he turned the box, pressing the runes in the sequence Kane indicated, then slid the key into the lock and turned it. Malyn was pretty sure he wasn't the only one holding his breath. There was an audible click, then Kieron rose and stepped back.

"Um…all yours," Kieron said backing up even farther.

Declan opened the box carefully. Even from where he was seated,

Malyn could see a square of folded parchment that had yellowed with age. Declan took it out of the box, unfolded it, and revealed a detailed map. "The Crypt of the Renounced. We needed the second key to get this map. We'll need the third key that Kane's going to steal to get into the crypt. I have a hunch that both the new keys and the gem will be needed to get the splinter of the crown. Offerings and gifts are customary for a journey into the underworld."

Malyn raised his eyebrows. "Underworld? That's a bit more than we bargained for, isn't it? Sounded like we were just raiding a tomb." Although, if he thought about it, he'd never believed it would be simple, not when the demigoddess chose a party that included someone of his skill and Declan's power.

"So the bag-of-needed-things gave us clothing and invitations," Malyn said, leaning back once more and closing his eyes. Even to his own ears, his voice sounded sleep-slurred. "Can you tell who they're for? Because it would be quite disappointing if I intended to go and the clothing is sized for Kieron or Mitchell." Both men were taller and bulkier than Malyn, who was lean and trim, but more slightly built even than Kane.

"Looks like they're right for you and me, which was the plan," Declan confirmed.

"You charm the Commissar with your fancy ways, Declan creates a disturbance, Mitchell and Kieron are the lookouts, and I steal what we need," Kane replied. "And hope this time, the treasure isn't spelled."

"Do we know anything about this 'Commissar' and why he has the key to the crypt? Or where to find it? I'd rather not ransack his whole house," Kane added.

"Check the book," Malyn directed without opening his eyes. He heard a bit of shuffling, then the rustle of pages as Declan did as he suggested.

"Huh. There are pages added that weren't here before," Declan said. "Notes on the Commissar and the floorplan to his house."

Malyn let out a sigh, glad that he wasn't the only one who could read the archaic language. Declan could handle this.

"Give us the quick summary," Kieron requested.

Declan was quiet for a while, and Malyn struggled to stay awake even with the curiosity of what Declan would share. Finally, he heard Declan shift and the snap as he closed the book.

"The Commissar is a collector of occult objects. He supposedly has quite a few on display in his house, but even more hidden away. The account says that just about any missing or legendary objects belong to him, although some of that is very likely exaggerated. However," Declan said, clearing his throat, "the book sounds quite clear about him having the key to the Crypt of the Renounced."

"Where?" Kane asked. "If I'm going to steal it, I need to know where to look."

"The Commissar has several keeping rooms where he stores his most precious objects. According to the map—which has a low-level enchantment on it—the key is here," he poked at the parchment. "The enchantment would tell us if he moved the key to another location."

"All right," Kane said, sounding somewhat appeased. "That's something. Does the book happen to say anything about how the keeping rooms are warded? Because I've never seen a collector who didn't safeguard his things."

Declan stayed quiet long enough that Malyn nearly drifted off. "The collector isn't a mage," he said. "He's got some minor ability, but nothing that would truly qualify him as a magic-user, or even a full witch. That might account for his obsession with magical objects, and his passion for anything occult."

"Compensating?" Kane's voice dripped with sarcasm.

"Perhaps," Declan murmured as if his full attention was elsewhere. "Or he might be the agent of someone who either does have magic and wishes to remain anonymous, or who wants to get those objects out of circulation."

"You don't think the Commissar intends to use the items in his collection?"

"Let's hope not. Some of the things rumored to be in his keeping room could cause big problems. I think if he had used any of them, there'd be a magical trace someone would have noticed."

The others continued to talk in low tones, but Malyn couldn't fight sleep any longer. He drifted off, utterly exhausted, hoping that by the time he woke his companions had a plan.

MALYN WOKE IN THE MORNING, surprised that his friends had let him sleep through his shift at watch. Even though he had not wholly recovered from the drain of the fight, he felt much improved.

"Any problems last night?" he asked, taking his portion of rations gratefully.

"There are always *things* abroad at night," Mitchell replied. "But compared to where we've just been? Nothing too bad."

Kane and Kieron stood off to one side, studying the road map. "We don't have very far to go," Kieron said. "About a half day's walk. I'm thinking that it might be worth the risk to take a room at an inn. We've been on the road for days. We'll all need to clean up before we try to go to a fancy party—as guests or thieves—and I, for one, could use a shave."

"Won't we attract attention?" Kane asked. "Four men and a half-elf female would certainly be unusual."

"If you keep your hood up and I cast a distraction spell, no one will notice," Declan said. "That kind of spell is such a common, minor magic, it won't be remarked on, either. But I agree that a shave would be much appreciated."

Malyn's beard didn't come in heavy, and it tended to be almost as white as his hair, but he preferred to be clean-shaven, and the unwanted beard itched. "I can check with the ghosts for a safe place to stop. Since it's daylight, we should be all right, what with ghost sentries and Declan's wards."

The idea of being able to stop in a real pub and wash away the grime of the road lifted everyone's spirits, and the group set out in a better mood than since they had left the Poxy Dragon. Kane and Kieron were in front, and Mitchell in the back. The sun shone, but without the heat that would come with summer. Other travelers passed with a tip of their hats or a greeting in passing, a much-appreciated reminder of normal.

A carriage passed, and the driver pointedly did not acknowledge their presence. Curtains covered the windows, so the passengers kept their anonymity, but also lost the ability to enjoy the beautiful day.

Long ago it had been Malyn in a carriage like that, the privileged son of a minor aristocrat. The third son, so not required to be either the heir or uphold the tradition of becoming a military officer. He thought he had managed to be unimportant enough to be overlooked, free to do as he wished. Still, his disinterest in both occupations and his talent for visions and speaking to the dead managed to disappoint his father and earn him the scorn of his older brothers. Healing was considered a blessing from the gods – speaking to the dead a curse that his father said brought shame on the family. His mother disagreed and had encouraged him, both in his academic pursuits and in his fashion choices.

Then she died, leaving no one to champion him.

So Malyn ran, leaving behind wealth, a noble name, and the privilege that came with it. He earned his keep as a hedge witch, healing and speaking to the dead for coin to put food in his belly and a roof over his head. Often he went hungry and slept rough. Still, he refused to give up his tattered silks and his kohl, or tone down his dramatic personality. It was all Malyn had left, of himself and of the things his mother had praised. Then a vision led him to Kieron, and ghosts led him to Declan. Malyn finally had the family he'd sought, and most of the time he could put the pain of his father's rejection out of his mind.

Now he headed to a party which was going to be full of men just like his father and brothers, and he feared that his old wounds were still raw.

"Are you worried about tonight?" Declan jarred Malyn from his brooding.

Malyn shrugged, not wanting to admit the path his thoughts had taken. "I expect it will be unpleasantly boring if we're lucky, and uncomfortably busy if we're not. And in between, we'll have to mingle with abominable pricks."

Declan laughed. "Don't mince words, Malyn. Tell me how you really feel."

Malyn grimaced and threw an obscene gesture. "We're not going to have fun. We're there to distract the man while Kane robs him. And while the book says he doesn't have magic, that doesn't mean he didn't purchase the services of a spellcaster to ward his belongings.

I've never met a collector who wasn't obsessively protective of his hoard." He shook his head. "They're like dragons."

"That's why I'm going with you," Declan replied. "Certainly not because of my social graces, although I shall try not to be an embarrassment."

Malyn snorted. "You'll be fine. I'll be the one they'll be talking about. I always am." As if his long white hair wasn't striking enough, the rest of his appearance and mannerisms tended to divide opinion. He clung to both defiantly, turning the reactions into a test of sorts. He'd learned long ago that it was better to know where he stood up front with people.

"You'll be spectacular, as always," Declan said with a chuckle. "Which will mean while they're all looking at you, no one will notice if my fingers are twitching or my lips are moving."

"I dare say, you'll have some admirers of your own." Malyn thought Declan's crow-black hair and bright blue eyes were striking, and the contrast between them doubly so.

"And we're still planning to spend the night at the lychgate after the job?" Malyn fretted. "Do you think that's wise, to be out in the open?"

"Lady Leota cautioned us to trust no one," Declan reminded him. "And the Commissar won't know what the rest of our party looks like, or have reason to think we have anything to do with the theft—if he notices anything missing. So no one will be looking for our group. But if anyone is suspicious, a pub that tells guards they've got strangers upstairs could do us in. We can hide in the lychgate."

"I suppose so," Malyn replied. "We've got the ghosts for protection."

"And my wardings and deflections. Don't forget, we're carrying a number of magical objects. They'll stand out at the pub if anyone knows to look, but the lychgate will help hide them."

"I've had more than my share of sleeping rough," Malyn said. "I like to avoid it when I can."

Declan chuckled. "Then take advantage to get a bit of shut-eye after you clean up, while the rest of us are at it. That'll likely have to do until we're home again."

They noted two pubs as they neared the market village of Bider. Both appeared to be reasonably prosperous, and the cooking smells that wafted toward the road made his stomach rumble in hunger. As they walked through the small town to check out the villa on the other side, Malyn sent out tendrils of his ghost magic to call nearby spirits, hoping to learn from them.

Declan kept a deflection spell up, just enough for them to be unremarkable to those they passed. Mitchell remained in his human form, but Malyn saw his nose twitch as he used his heightened sense of smell to gain information. Kane had the hood of her cloak up so that the Elven cast to her features and ears would not be noticed, but Malyn felt certain she was taking in every detail.

That left Kieron to interact with the locals, which was his usual role when they did jobs back in Kortufan. Kieron might not have magic, but he could turn on his charm when needed, winning the help of women and the good-natured support of men. Declan had sworn to Malyn that Kieron's charisma was natural and not a trick of magic or the aura of an amulet.

Kieron's gift is quite a valuable talent, Malyn thought. Particularly since Declan tended to be withdrawn and awkward in a crowd, while Malyn was remarked upon and Kane tended to just tell the world to screw itself. Mitchell was the next most social of them, ironic since wolf shifters were not known for playing well with others.

Not much happens here.

'Twas boring in life, worse in death.

Nothing changes. They just go on without us.

Malyn found the ghosts' voices both reassuring and melancholy. They seemed resigned to their lot here, those that had not chosen to move on. At the least, he thought, the ghosts weren't telling tales of murder and rampage. When he sent out questions about the Commissar, the ghosts said only that he lived in the big house and kept to himself, having everything he needed delivered and almost never being seen in the village.

"Anything?" he asked Declan in a low tone as they passed through town and headed up the road that led near the Villa of the Commissar. They all wanted to get the lay of the land before tonight's event.

Kieron, Kane, and Mitchell talked about the road and side roads, the best approach, and the height of the wall that surrounded the villa. Malyn and Declan used their abilities to search out any advantages, magical or ghostly.

"There's a basic protection spell on the wall, nothing I can't disrupt," Declan said. "There's also a containment spell inside the wall. I don't think it's to keep people in. I think it's to blunt the magic of all the items he's collected. From what's leaking out, despite the spell, I'd say he has a very interesting collection of objects that have real power."

"I was hoping he was a fraud," Malyn confessed. "One who got lucky and accidentally picked up a real relic among the shiny trash."

"No such luck," Declan replied. "On the bright side, the energy doesn't feel too terribly dark. Nothing like Nightshade Monastery. Definitely some dangerous pieces—I can feel them straining at the containment—but most just feel odd."

"Well, he *is* a collector," Malyn said. "That's what might appeal to him. The odd, the rare, the unique. If he doesn't have magic, he might be rather 'deaf' to the energy."

"It's hard to imagine anyone—even without a scrap of magic—being 'deaf' to those vibrations," Declan answered, shuddering. "But I imagine it's possible."

"I went to a museum once when I was young," Malyn said. "In the palace city, with my father. It was like a library, but with all kinds of artifacts from places far away, and relics from long ago. There were even bodies, preserved in the peat bog that had been put out for display. He didn't believe me when I said that the ghosts were all around us, sad and angry. But they were."

Malyn's voice grew quiet. "So many of the pieces on display had power. I didn't really know what it was then, just that they made me itchy or screamed in my mind. But hundreds of visitors like my father went as a diversion. It didn't bother them at all."

"Kind of like going to hear musicians and not hearing a note," Declan said.

"Which means it makes even more sense for Kieron to go in with Kane," Malyn agreed. "Mitchell will keep watch. We'll hear him howl, and he can outrun anyone who sees him and decides to give chase. But if the Commissar has items in his collection that cause problems for Kane, Kieron might not be affected. He can get the key and get her out."

Declan's gaze flicked to where Kane was deep in conversation with the others. "I wouldn't suggest to Kane that she might need to be rescued if I were you. At least, if I were you and wanted to keep my plums."

Malyn smiled. "I like my plums right where they are, thank you."

The villa was screened from view by a high wall and slender, stately trees. Still, they could get a sense of the size of the compound and the best ways in and out. Malyn inwardly lamented that they were on foot for this quest, since if the Commissar or his guards realized the theft, they would be limited on how far and fast they could flee.

Still, the demigoddess had outfitted them, and perhaps the lack of horses reflected a vote of confidence in their abilities. Malyn preferred options, and short of horse thievery, their choices were limited.

Back in town, they chose the Cock and Bull tavern for their lodgings, though they had no intent to spend the night. Kane kept her hood up, and no one paid the group any mind as they trudged up the stairs carrying extra buckets of water.

"Considering some of the places we've been, this isn't bad." Kane's lukewarm praise amounted to a ringing endorsement from her.

"If there aren't rats in my bed or in our dinner, I count it a win," Kieron said, eyeing with envy the bed with its lumpy straw mattress.

"We've got three buckets to clean up with, and a bed that should hold three people, plus a chair," Mitchell said. "I propose three of us get cleaned up, then lie down while the other two wash. Then we swap, and the first three keep watch. We've got a few candlemarks to spare before the event."

His suggestion met rousing approval, and Malyn was happy to doze when he finished getting ready. It felt good to wipe the worst of the road dirt from his skin and make his hair presentable.

He smoothed his hands over the fabric of the clothing the demigoddess had provided, enjoying the feel of it. Growing up, he'd taken for granted clothing of the finest fabrics and latest styles, with a wardrobe full of outfits, and new ones added each season. His mother had indulged his passion for brightly colored silks and satins, instead of the dark colors and more practical fabrics preferred by his father and brothers. She had also encouraged him to play up his eyes with kohl and add some color to his pale skin with a hint of rouge or by biting his lips to pink them.

When he had fled his father's house, he'd taken only what he could carry. On the streets, fine fabrics weren't durable, and the way he stood out had earned him a beating or two before he discovered how to call the ghosts to protect him. Malyn learned to blend in, avoid notice. But even at the worst, he'd kept a bright scarf or a waistcoat to tether him to who he was. And when he had a bit of coin more than needed to pay his share of the rent, food, and kindling, Malyn frequented the merchants who traded in cast-off clothing, happy to secure some finer pieces. Once he felt safe with Kieron and the others, he dared use the kohl once more, and on feast days a bit of rouge for celebration. They had never mocked him, nor had the ghosts, another reason Malyn considered his companions more kin than his blood family.

On the road he'd toned down his appearance, taking a light hand with the kohl and choosing more subdued colors, the better to be unremarkable to anyone they passed. Lady Leota, however, had other plans. Malyn had been almost giddy when he had unwrapped the clothing from the pack. A fine emerald green silk shirt and black trousers over a pair of soft black leather shoes would make the most of his hair and coloring, and coordinated well with the blue satin shirt the demigoddess provided for Declan. He hoped that the clothing did not vanish when the night was over, because he had every intention of taking it back with him and wearing it on feast days until the pieces fell apart.

Kane, Mitchell, and Kieron were not supposed to be seen, so they hadn't received new outfits, but the chance to wash and attend to grooming still made them much more presentable, and less likely to be spotted as vagrants. Malyn had enjoyed every minute of his shave, a task he usually found annoying. Now, rested and dressed to impress, Malyn felt more like himself, enough to gather his confidence before walking into an event he dreaded.

They gathered their packs and headed out well in advance,

giving them time to walk to the villa and stash their belongings where they could be retrieved in a hurry. The cool day and light breeze made the walk pleasant and kept them from working up too much of a sweat.

"The other guests are likely to arrive by carriage," Malyn noted as he and Declan approached the house. "So we can't show up sweating like farmhands."

"Another reason we're going early," Declan said. "And we'll tell them that our coach left us off down the lane because one of the horses was feeling poorly." He raised an eyebrow. "No one wants a sick horse taking a dump outside their mansion."

Kane, Kieron, and Mitchell had taken a different route, circling around to the back where they could enter through the servants' door.

Keep an eye on my friends, and let me know if they have problems, Malyn instructed the ghosts who had answered his call.

"Do you know who they are? The ghosts?" Declan asked as they strolled up the lane.

"One is Millie, a servant who died a while back and wasn't in a hurry to move on. The other is Helena, a cousin who was visiting and died of a fever."

"And they don't have any conflict being your lookouts?"

Malyn shrugged. "I explained that we needed the key to save lives. They were agreeable. And they can go places Mitchell and Kieron can't."

"I've got a few tricks in mind if we need a diversion," Declan replied. "Smile. It's time to put on our show."

The villa with its marble columns and parquet floor was bigger and grander than Malyn had thought from the glimpse he'd gotten. The white facade gleamed in the torchlight, while candles lit up the large windows. Inside, the Commissar's eccentric tastes became clear in furnishings that mixed and matched time periods, styles, and kingdoms of origin. Huge bouquets of fresh flowers made the rooms smell like a garden. Despite it all, the mishmash worked, and Malyn felt a few seconds of regret over having to steal from a man whose interests suggested he might be fascinating.

"Ambassador Taurean, from the kingdom of Herendon," the page announced, reading aloud from Malyn's invitation. "And his attaché," he added, noting Declan.

Malyn managed to keep from smirking, and swept into the grand hall with Declan a step behind. The subterfuge gave Declan more freedom to watch the crowd and listen for problems with his magic, while Malyn played the role he was truly born to play.

That observation was too spot on for Malyn's comfort as he strode into the crowd. Old training and habits came back unbidden, and he squared his shoulders, standing straight, and lifting his chin in the same arrogant expression he had loathed on his father. It made him fit in here, among people he immediately judged, by their jewels and apparel, to be his family's noble equals.

"So pleased you could join us, Ambassador." The Commissar, a well-fed man, dressed in an immaculate silk shirt, brocade vest, satin breeches, and velvet frock coat, thrust out a beefy hand to shake Malyn's.

"The pleasure is mine," Malyn replied smoothly and made a perfect bow.

"You have done me an honor, traveling so far. I trust your journey has been pleasant?"

"It's always exciting to see the sights of a foreign land," Malyn answered, figuring it to be the most truthful thing he would utter all night.

"Good. Good. We'll talk later. Now, I must see to my other guests. Please avail yourself—the brandy is excellent, and my cook has outdone himself with the cakes and savories." The Commissar waved a hand toward the side of the room, where tables laden with delicacies awaited, and servants moved among the guests bearing trays with goblets of wine and brandy.

Declan leaned close when the Commissar walked away. "Most of the decorative objects in this room either have a magical residue or have a supernatural resonance. Can you feel it?"

Malyn nodded. "Not dangerous. But distracting."

He and Declan made their way over to the banquet table, stopping along their path to exchange pleasantries with strangers. Malyn felt certain that Lady Leota had chosen a foreign kingdom so that "Ambassador Taurean" would be unlikely to run into anyone who could actually recognize him if such a person really existed.

Malyn looked around the gathering as he took his time nibbling a small cake filled with a tangy, unfamiliar fruit. He was not acquainted with anyone in the room, and yet he felt as if he knew all of them intimately, their secrets and petty jealousies, their ambitions and grievances, their cold passions and hot rage. The faces didn't matter; he'd grown up with their ilk, been bred to walk among them as an equal.

For a time, after he fled his father's wrath, Malyn wanted vindication, if not exactly vengeance. He'd run with little more than the clothes on his back, and in those first hungry, desperate days, his solace lay in the fantasy that one day, when he had earned notice as a powerful healer-psychic, a medium of renown, maybe even a necromancer, he would achieve such acclaim that his stiff-necked father and stone-faced brothers would be forced to acknowledge his worth and their mistake.

But as time passed, he discovered that he was all right with where he'd landed, and the freedom it afforded him to be exactly who he wanted to be. Malyn gazed at the guests at the party, all of them wealthy, titled, and powerful—and none of them free.

Malyn made small talk with those who approached him, knowing that with his hair, kohl-rimmed eyes and bright silks, he cut a fine figure.

Declan hung back, listening and appraising, keeping tabs with his magic on what transpired elsewhere, with Kane and Kieron. Since the other attendees saw Declan as Malyn's assistant, and therefore not their equal, he was effectively invisible, leaving him free to craft his back-up spells. Malyn checked in with his ghost lookouts and started to relax when nothing seemed amiss.

That was, of course, a mistake.

"Ambassador." The Commissar had made his way around the room and now found his way back to Malyn. "A word, if you please."

"Of course," Malyn replied, inclining his head in assent. He followed the big man to a table off to one side. Tacit understanding must have deemed the table to be for more discreet conversations, since the chatting crowd had not claimed it, and those standing and talking gave them space enough for a semblance of privacy.

"I seek your guidance about an item I am most anxious to acquire," the Commissar said, settling his bulk into one of the chairs. Malyn perched on the edge of his seat, while Declan stood behind him, playing his role as assistant and protector.

"How may I be of service?" Malyn hated how easily the gracious phrases and affectations came back to him, how naturally the words rolled off his tongue and his body reverted to its original training.

The Commissar reached into his vest and produced a paper, which he unfolded and laid out flat in front of Malyn. "I desire the ankle bones of King Leonard," he said, showing a sketch of an ornate box covered in runes. "They are said to have healing properties, and I was hoping that being from Herendon, you would be familiar with them."

Now that Malyn had time to study his host, he saw the signs of illness: a sallow cast to the skin, trembling hands, and a blotchy complexion. His wealth and collections could only do so much for the illness that threatened him.

"I have heard of the relic," Malyn replied. "It's prized by its current owner. I was not aware it was for sale."

"Everything is for sale, for the right price."

Close up, Malyn saw the fear in the man's eyes. He wondered how many of the items in the Commissar's collection were to stave off one sort of misfortune or another, a bulwark against fate.

"I will make inquiries," Malyn said with his most charming, least sincere, smile. "But I cannot promise."

"I must have that relic," the Commissar said, leaning into Malyn's space. "I don't have time to waste."

Malyn shifted back. "I understand your urgency, but I do not control—"

"You couldn't possibly understand," the Commissar snapped. "It's not my time yet. I have much more to do."

And I'm sure the current owner feels the same way. "I will do what I can," Malyn said.

Malyn's ghost spies pinged his mind, warning of danger. He scratched his left ear, a signal to Declan. Declan brushed a hand against

Malyn's shoulder, letting him know the message was received. Malyn felt Declan's power shift and knew he was getting ready in case they needed to launch a distraction.

"I should have known you were just for show," the Commissar said, starting to rise. "I need to talk to someone with real power."

How typical, Malyn thought. As soon as he had been determined to be of no value, he too, like Declan, became invisible to the Commissar. The man was just like Malyn's father.

Malyn caught a glimpse of motion and saw a guard approaching. He called out to the ghosts, as Declan tensed, and loosed his magic.

You wanted "real" power? This is what it looks like.

A sudden chill fell over the room, going in the space of a heartbeat from the warmth of a crowd to a cold so bracing the guests could see their breath. An unseen force swept through the dangling crystal teardrops on the huge chandelier overhead, causing a glissando of tinkling glass. The candles extinguished, plunging the room into darkness, then lit anew, with flames that jumped a foot into the air above each wax pillar.

The crowd exclaimed in awe at first, thinking it all an entertainment, then gasped at the flare of fire, as it dawned on them that this was not part of the plan. Silvery witch orbs appeared, dancing and darting in the air, beautiful until they began to dive at individual guests, effectively herding them toward the doors.

Green foxfire glowed just beyond the windows, tempting the guests to follow it into the darkness, toward the lawn maze and gardens. The ghost of a young woman appeared in the doorway, translucent, flickering like a flame in a breeze.

"What is going on?" The Commissar rose from his seat, growing red in the face. "I demand to know right now!"

Guests screamed and panicked. Some ran from the room, while others tried desperately to open windows when they saw the ghost. The orbs chased the attendees back and forth across the room, swooping and diving at their heads. In their panic, some of them blundered into the table of food, knocking it to the ground in a clash and clatter of serving dishes. A candelabra fell, igniting the heavy curtains, which went up in flames with a roar.

"Uh oh," Declan murmured at the unexpected turn the diversion had taken.

The Commissar waded out into the chaos, screaming for servants to put out the blaze and coaxing frightened guests not to stampede. No one seemed to be listening.

Malyn closed his eyes, concentrating on the ghosts watching over Kane and Kieron. Even with the floorplan, finding the key must have taken longer than expected, because they clearly needed more time.

Declan made a subtle gesture toward the flaming draperies, using his magic to seize control of the fire. "It's contained," he whispered to Malyn. "But it won't go out until I will it."

Just a bit longer. You're doing great, Malyn sent to his mischievous ghosts. They were enjoying the havoc, the closest the spirits had been to feeling alive in many years. None of the ghosts hurt the guests. Instead, they appeared out of nowhere directly in front of people, eliciting piercing screams and causing several to faint. Word spread among the restless ghosts of the villa, because more came to join the fun, rattling shutters, shattering a mirror, and knocking small items from shelves and tables.

"Not that statue!" the Commissar screamed, darting faster than a Malyn thought a man of his size would be able to move, launching himself into the air to snatch a precious figurine out of the air, and clutching it to his bosom as he landed hard on his shoulder and hip, which sent a shudder through the whole room.

The nudge of a corpse-cold, invisible finger told Malyn that Kane and Kieron were making their way out the back.

"We're through," he murmured to Declan, who seemed to be enjoying making faces appear in the flaming curtains, much to the horror of the frightened guests.

"If you say so," Declan replied with an exaggerated sigh. He made a complicated set of movements with his fingers, directed at the draperies. "We can go," he said, tugging on Malyn's arm.

"Must we burn the villa to the ground?"

"We won't. It's not a real fire now. It's a fire daemon, a sentient creature beholden to me. He'll go on performing for another little bit, then vanish. The 'fire' will go out with no additional damage, and we'll be long gone."

Kane and Kieron had studied the floor plan to know where in the Commissar's vast storage rooms to find the key. Malyn had memorized them for a different purpose—escape. With the ghosts and the daemon "entertaining" the guests at the front of the house, he and Declan couldn't leave the way they came. Instead, he led Declan through the back corridors, not bothering to explain himself to the servants who looked askance at them, silencing any potential questions from the guards with an imperious jerk of his head.

The narrow corridor spilled out into the back of the villa, near the garbage pit, by the smell of it, Malyn thought. Much as he hated the thought of damaging his new clothing with sweat, he and Declan kept a steady jog through the cool night, taking a winding path through the woodlands back to where they left their packs.

"Where are they?" Declan said, short of breath. "You said they had already left? What if they were caught?"

Even at this distance, Malyn's connection to the spirits held. "They're not in the house. Maybe they had to take a longer route. The ghosts are still keeping the party going. Their new game is knocking trinkets off the shelves and throwing them across the room to make the Commissar fetch."

Declan gave him a sidelong glance. "You're enjoying this a little too much."

Malyn sighed. "Until tonight, there was always a little part of me that thought someday I'd walk back into my father's house dripping in silks and diamonds, with all kinds of accolades from people he thought were important, that I'd redeem myself. Or, better, make him admit he was wrong."

"And now?"

"I realize that his opinion doesn't matter. It never did. And no matter what, I don't want that life. It wouldn't be any better than I remember it, and all the privileges come with a cost. Did you see the people at that party tonight? They had less life to them than the ghosts."

"So that means you'll stay when we get our farm?" Declan's genuine smile warmed Malyn's cynical heart.

"Yes, I suppose," he said, with a dramatic flourish to lighten the moment. A wolf's howl drew their attention to where three shadowy figures cut through the woods toward them.

"They're here. Time for us to leave." He sent his thanks to the ghosts of the villa, shouldered his pack, and headed down the road.

DECLAN

"ARE YOU PICKING UP ANYTHING?" MITCHELL ASKED, LOOKING OVER Declan's shoulder as he unwrapped the items Kane and Kieron had risked so much to retrieve. "For all the bother, shouldn't they look more special?"

Declan carefully tipped the velvet bag, letting the long chain pool, followed by an amulet and matching key. He agreed; they didn't impress. They were both of simple iron. The unusual stylized skull and bones depicted on the amulet were repeated on the handle of the key.

"First rule of magic—the things that don't look important are usually the most dangerous," Declan said.

"Seriously? That's the first rule of magic?" Kieron questioned.

"No. The first rule of magic is don't touch strange books or objects unless you want to turn into a toad," Declan replied. He handled the key by the soft cloth it came wrapped in, unwilling to touch the metal until he had thoroughly checked for unwanted extras like curses or bound spirits. To his relief, a scan with his magic declared the key to be…just a key.

"If it's not magic and there's nothing special about them, why go to all the bother of hiding them away? Why would a guy like the

Commissar want an old key and an ugly amulet?" Mitchell stared at the items as if they might do tricks if he watched long enough.

"Collectors want things with notoriety, or that come from a famous place. The Crypt of the Renounced is pretty famous," Malyn observed. "Some people say it's the gateway to the underworld."

"Is it really?" Kieron looked worried. "Those stories we read about the gods and monsters, none of their trips to the underworld ever went well."

"I've never been there, so I only know what I've read," Declan replied. "It's not a place to take lightly. And from what I've heard, there's more than one gateway, if you can believe the sources."

"The key may also activate dormant magic when it's united with its lock," Malyn said. "I've heard of spells like that. The magic is in the lock, but it's triggered by the presence of a special object—like the key. So only that particular key—not a copy or a lock pick—will do."

"And the amulet?" Kieron asked skeptically.

"No idea—" Declan said, poking at the items.

"They may also have been given to the Commissar by someone with a motive to keep them hidden. His collection is certainly a place to make sure something stays lost," Kane added, her dislike of the collector's archives clear in her voice.

"We had floor plans of the monastery and the Commissar's collection room," Mitchell mused. "And we have a map to get us to the crypt —but do we happen to have a map of whatever lies inside the crypt?"

Malyn reached into the food bag for the book and turned to the back. New writing had appeared on the last page.

"Two guards, two gifts," Malyn read aloud. "An implacable foe stands watch over what you seek. Best him and the splinter of the crown is yours." He looked up. "There's more here, about the crypt and who actually ended up renounced and from what."

"What is it with deities that they can't say things straight out?" Kieron grumbled. "Always riddles."

"I think that's part of the quest," Kane replied. "Proof that we're smart enough to figure things out, the way everything is a test to make sure we're worthy."

"Are we?" Declan asked, looking up, meeting their eyes.

"You think we're not?" Mitchell challenged.

Declan frowned. "I don't...I'm not..." He faltered, then found what he was searching for. "We're mercenaries. We're not from Sorenden, and so whatever happens to its king or to the whole kingdom doesn't really affect us. We're not here to save them. I don't know about you, but I haven't given them a second thought. Maybe they're dying. Maybe they're starving. We don't know, and we don't really care. We're here for the gold, to build a farm that will solve our problems. Is that worthy?"

"No shame in doing a job for pay," Kieron replied. "What we do with the pay is our business, isn't it? I'm more apt to trust a fellow who wants a bit of coin for his effort than one who wants me to believe he's some kind of hero."

"If we had to be from Sorenden to reclaim the splinter, don't you think Lady Leota would have arranged that?" Kane said. "After all, apparently people come from far and wide to the Poxy Dragon to prove that they're heroes. For all we know, maybe some Sorenden folks came and failed, and now we have to clean up their bloody mess."

"I wish we knew more about the 'implacable foe,'" Declan admitted. "That could be so many things, all with different spells to deal with them. I just want to be prepared."

"Whatever happens, we've got your back," Kieron assured him. "We got this far. We'll figure it out. And then we'll use that first key in the next lychgate to go home."

Declan smiled, unwilling to bring down the spirits of his companions, but he felt certain it would not be that simple. Perhaps they knew that truth as well and were all bluffing.

Everyone made an effort to keep the conversation light as they ate their rations. "I think that the first thing I want when we get home is a meat pie," Kieron said and washed down a bite of sausage with a swig of wine.

"I'd like a fruit tart or a bit of mincemeat pie," Malyn added with a sigh. "Haven't had either in quite a while."

"Maybe some roasted lamb." Kane didn't take her eyes off the road outside the lychgate. "It reminds me of the food back where I came from." Declan noticed that she very carefully did not call that place "home."

"A nice raw hunk of beef would suit me," Mitchell said with a toothy grin. "Wouldn't even mind if I had to hunt it myself. Of course, I'd share the bounty." He glanced at Declan. "How about you?"

"I'm rather partial to lemon cake," he said wistfully. "Hard to come by, but very good." Declan didn't add that he hadn't had any of that cake since he'd left the order of mages he'd once been part of, before his failure damaged his magic, before they cast him out. The memory was bittersweet and left him melancholy.

"When we have the farm up and running, we won't go hungry. We can grow our own food, raise livestock, plant fruit trees. Trade for what we can't grow or make ourselves. There'll be plenty of wood for the fire so we won't be cold, flax and wool to spin and weave," Kieron said. "We just have one more task to complete, and the gold is ours."

And the burden of that task fell to Declan. He felt the weight and responsibility like a leaden yoke. His friends were counting on him not just to protect them and help everyone get home safely, but to win them the future Kieron laid out as their reward. Declan wanted that future so badly his teeth ached, and the thought that it all fell to him to make it happen had him close to panic.

I can't do this. I couldn't do it the last time, and so why would I think I can now? I nearly died. What if I die? How can the others complete the quest? Oh gods, I'm not the one. Why did I agree to come? My magic isn't what it used to be. How could anyone think I'd be up to a battle in the underworld?

The others continued to joke and laugh about the food and drink they wanted most. Malyn laid a hand on Declan's arm. "You all right?"

Declan felt sure his misery showed in his face, but he just swallowed hard and gave a sharp nod. "Sure. I'm fine."

"You know, I'd feel better if we went over the new portion of the book," Malyn said, not making eye contact. "I'd like to know everything I can about the ghosts down there, because it's the underworld and there are going to be dead things. Maybe between the two of us, we can figure out a plan."

Declan managed a wan smile, appreciative of Malyn's offer and roundabout way of trying to head off his worries. "That would be good. I think we should do that."

"Listen up, everyone." The group turned to look at Malyn. "We need to figure out how we're going to handle the crypt. I'll read from the book, and then we decide who's doing what. I, for one, have no desire to end up stuck in the underworld because we didn't mind the details."

Malyn took the book out of the rations bag and leaned back against one of the benches where the light was best from their shuttered lantern. Kane and Mitchell were on duty, and remained looking out over the road and the graveyard, though nothing had stirred since they had reached the lychgate.

"First, once we're done, how far to the next lychgate so we can go home?" Malyn asked Kieron.

Kieron unrolled the map and studied it for a moment. "Just a couple of miles. The closest one to the crypt is beyond it, instead of backtracking."

"Good to know," Malyn replied. He paged through to the end. "According to this, the Crypt of the Renounced holds the bodies of Estan of Agivar and his two sons. He was a liegeman and mage to an ancient king, but he and his sons betrayed the king in battle to win favor from a necromancer, who promised he could make Estan's dead wife live again. But the gods were angered by Estan's faithlessness and with the necromancer for misusing his powers. They smote the necromancer, but they condemned Estan and his sons to become the watchmen of the Final Shore."

Malyn frowned as he read on. "One of the sons was turned into a large bird that guards the door. The second was turned into an old man with failing memory who asks questions of any who seek to pass. Estan himself was doomed to be the guardian of the waters, the gatekeeper the dead must pass in order to enter the Afterlife."

"Just to be clear, we don't actually have to go into the Afterlife, right?" Kieron clarified.

"I haven't gotten to that part yet," Malyn said, sounding slightly miffed at being interrupted. He found his place and went back to reading. "There's a note here that says that the splinter of the crown was

hidden on the Final Shore by the thief who stole it. He had an enchantment that allowed him to carry it as far as the shore before Estan forced
him to give it up in order to move on." He looked up. "So we have to
either evade or fight Estan to get to the splinter."

"He's a ghost. You've fought ghosts before," Mitchell said.

Malyn shook his head. "Estan isn't just a ghost. He's a mage. And it
looks like the gods let him keep his powers." He looked at Declan. "We
can bribe the sons, but when the thief brought the splinter to the Final
Shore, Estan now considers it his. You'll have to duel him to get it back,
and get us out alive."

Declan tried to hide his emotions, but Malyn's words made him
panic. He had done everything in his power to leave the past and his
failures behind, and now the quest placed him squarely in line to do
what he had sworn he would never do again.

The others debated the fine points of dealing with the guardians
and the path to take to the Final Shore. Declan's world narrowed to the
chaos of his thoughts and the pounding of his heart, the rapid rise and
fall of his breath. He thought he might pass out from hyperventilating
or throw up. Neither one would inspire confidence.

*Maybe they shouldn't have confidence in me. I'm not who I was—or what
I used to be. Gods, please don't let me get them all killed.*

If he had a choice, Declan would have backed out and insisted they
find someone else. But here they were, far from home in a foreign land.
There was no substitute. Either Declan did his part, or the quest failed.
Both possibilities made his heart seize.

After a while, the conversation lagged, and they chose who would
take first watch while the others slept. They spent the night under the
protection of the lychgate, which Declan augmented with the warded
rope and the addition of deflection spells to avert the attention of
passers-by. Malyn called to the ghosts of the graveyard to protect them
and alert them to danger, and now that they were out of the Deadlands
and the Shadow Woods, the ghosts were agreeable to oblige.

Malyn and he drew the second watch, which suited Declan just
fine. The night grew quiet except for the hoots of owls and the occa-
sional rustle of nocturnal creatures, normal and supernatural. None of
them bothered the wards around the lychgate or seemed to pay its

occupants any attention. Which gave Declan far too much time to worry.

"This is really upsetting you, isn't it?" Malyn said quietly. The others were sound asleep, and the lychgate wasn't very wide, so they could speak in low tones.

Declan nodded. "I'm sorry. It's just that, the last time, things didn't go well."

Malyn gave him an appraising look. Declan expected pity or disgust. Instead, he saw only concern, which seemed worse. Pity or disgust he could fight against. Concern broke him. "That was last time. You're a different person now. It doesn't have to go the same way."

Declan swallowed hard. "But what if it does?"

Malyn didn't ask what had happened in the past, which made Declan somehow more willing to tell him. "I was at the collegium, in my final year. I witnessed one of the older students trading in dark magical objects. He went after me and we ended up dueling. I was just trying to protect myself, but he intended to kill me to keep me quiet. We were equally skilled, but he was willing to use lethal magic, forbidden magic. I was able to deflect the worst of the strike and wound him badly enough to stop the duel, but pulling that much power without the right grounding nearly killed me and shattered my magic."

"And your attacker?"

Declan looked away. "He blamed me, said I struck first. I was in no shape to tell my side of the story, and he came from a powerful family. Besides, I was useless to the collegium at that point, since my magic was broken. They threw me out. You know how it went from there."

Malyn did know, because he'd been the one to find Declan and bring him into the circle of friends when he was barely able to call hand fire or light a candle. Declan knew that Malyn had been doing everything in his power to help him heal since.

"I've seen what you can do since you're in a better place," Malyn said. "And I know how that kind of stuff can mess with your mind and make you doubt your power. But you're a good mage, Declan. You can do this."

Declan gave a bitter snort. "You mean, we're all screwed if I can't, so you really, really hope I can do this. I get that. I know. And I won't let you down. I'll figure it out."

"If there's anything the rest of us can do to help you prepare, just say so," Malyn urged. "You don't have to do it alone, if there's another option."

"Let me think about it," Declan said. "I just...can't right now."

Malyn wisely said nothing, and they sat out the rest of their watch in silence. Declan's thoughts went round and round, and much as he tried not to dwell on the failure in the past, it haunted his present just like the ghosts that begged for Malyn's attention.

Finally, just as the sun peeked over the horizon, Declan finally came to a conclusion. *I am probably healed sufficiently to hold my own while the others steal the splinter of the crown. I'll hold off Estan while they escape. Once they're gone, it won't matter if I fail, or burn up trying. They'll have the splinter, and gold enough for the farm. And I'll have done my duty.*

Oddly, once he accepted his fate, the weight lifted, and Declan found his mood much improved. His cold breakfast of sausage, bread, and cheese tasted better than he remembered. Declan paid attention to the banter of his companions, committing their faces and voices to memory, basking in their company. If this was to be his last day, then he did not intend to waste it in worry or sorrow, and he would not let his friends dwell on his sacrifice. Instead, he found joy listening to their daydreams of the farm Declan did not expect to live to see. The happiness in their faces made the reward worth the cost.

Funny, Declan thought, *how knowing the end is near makes everything stand out so sharply.* As they walked, he could have sworn that the colors of the birds and plants, the smell of the air, the feel of the breeze was so much more vivid than before. Perhaps it was because he had finally thrown off the darkness that dogged his thoughts, even if it was just for one singular day. Declan's shoulders lost their tension, and he smiled and laughed with the group, though he let them do the talking.

Kane and Kieron were in front, as usual, and Mitchell brought up the rear. Malyn and Declan walked together in the middle, sometimes discussing the magic necessary for the crypt, or remarking on the landscape as they walked.

Several candlemarks into the journey, Malyn gave him an

appraising look. "Don't take this the wrong way, but you're in an awfully good mood."

Declan smiled, and for once it was completely genuine. "I'm glad that it's all nearly over. Once we finish at the crypt, it's back to the Poxy Dragon, and then to our farm." He did not think it necessary to add that he likely wouldn't be joining them.

Something flickered in Malyn's eyes, but his smile held. "Yeah. It'll be good to get home. I'm grateful for the trail rations, but there's only so much cheese and sausage I can eat."

Thankfully, Malyn did not press for more conversation. Declan wanted to soak up the feel of the sunlight and the movement of the clouds, all of the details of life around him and hold them in his mind. He didn't know if he'd have his memories in the afterlife, but if he did, then he wanted to remember this day and his friends, just like this.

They had passed few travelers once they left the last town, and it was some distance yet to the next village. The few riders or peddlers who did pass them paid no mind and went on their way with a nod. After a while, Kieron and Kane slowed and consulted the map.

"We're close," Kieron said. "There should be a lane leading off the road, heading toward the ruins of an old manor. Estan's manor," he added. "The Crypt of the Renounced is Estan's family's mausoleum."

"Once again, proof that the gods have a dark sense of humor," Malyn observed.

"From what you read in the book, there may be additional protections around the crypt," Mitchell warned. "I don't think the gods really want company."

"We'll deal with it." Kieron rolled up the map and stuffed it into his pack. "Come on. Not much longer."

An overgrown carriage path led off from the main road, winding through an honor guard of tall trees in straight rows on either side. The trees and a low stone wall were the only real clues to where the old path lay, since it had obviously not been used for a very long time. They left the highway with reluctance, heading into the thicket. In the distance, Declan could barely make out a hill, and he wondered if the ruins sat at the crest. That might work for the old manor, but the crypt was likely to be a distance away, where it wouldn't mar the view.

"I should have brought a bush knife," Kieron muttered as they fought through vines and thorn bushes. Declan thought it likely that the path to the old manor had purposely been magicked to be nearly impassable to keep out the curiosity seekers who came looking because of old legends.

Kane easily scaled a tree to get the details that the map omitted. "The house must have been on the hill. But the road forks at the base. That's where the map said to go right, toward the crypt," she reported when she rejoined them.

"I'm not picking up anything heading our way," Mitchell said, turning to sniff the air. "But there are creatures watching us. Can't tell what kind. They're keeping their distance—for now."

"Do you think the items we've acquired might work as passage tokens for this part?" Malyn asked. "Showing that we have a reason to be here?"

"Let's hope so," Kieron replied, wiping the sweat from his forehead. "I'd really rather not have to fight my way in—just to fight again inside."

The thorns and vines held no enchantment—Declan checked. That did not make them any easier to cross through. Brambles caught at their pants and tore at exposed flesh. Tendrils and runners threatened to trip them with every step. Insects rose from the brush as they disturbed it, forming a biting, stinging cloud. The good mood of earlier in the day vanished, replaced with sweat and curses.

Declan refused to let the challenges bother him. It was a small thing, in the grand scheme of it all, and not what he wished to remember.

When they passed the turn that would have led to the grand home, Declan followed the path up to the crest and studied what he could see of the crumbling building. It must have been impressive in its day, probably a castle more than a mansion. He could only imagine what it might have looked like, but from the size of the foundation it had been very large. *A shame that it came to ruin because of the faithlessness of its owner.*

"Are there ghosts?" he asked Malyn.

Malyn looked up, eyebrows furrowed and mouth set in a hard line.

He had a streak of dirt on one cheek and leaves caught in his hair. In other circumstances, Declan would have laughed.

"Nothing that's coming after us, thank the gods," he said. "But yes, any time you're at a site this old, there are ghosts. They seem happy to watch us from afar. I don't think anyone's been this way for a long time."

Finally, the Crypt of the Renounced came into view. Declan had expected a temple-like building, maybe a shrine. The gray stone building had few flourishes, save the excellent workmanship of its stonemasons. It was the size of a modest house, though Declan knew from the maps that its real size was much larger, since it extended far underground. The structure had a domed roof and intricately carved gargoyles and grotesques guarded each corner. Two narrow, barred windows let in some light and air, at least to the antechamber.

A raven's caw broke the silence, and the shadow of wings slipped over them in the instant before the dark bird dove at them with remarkable speed. It was at least twice the size of a regular raven, with a sharp-looking beak and wicked talons. Again and again, the over-sized raven swooped and plummeted, catching at hair and striking at ears and faces.

"It's the first guardian!" Declan shouted, as he waved his arms frantically to keep the bird from striking him. He did not want to use magic against it, since they required the guardian's permission to enter the crypt. He doubted the keeper would feel generous after he blasted it out of the sky—assuming his magic would even work against a god-cursed being like Estan's son.

"Keep him off me, and I'll get the stone!" Kieran yelled. He dropped to a crouch, huddled over his pack, while Kane and Mitchell waved their arms and cloaks. Despite their efforts, the raven had scored several hits.

"Hurry up! Blood draws attention!" Mitchell shouted. Mitchell bled from a gash on his temple and Kane a gouge on her forearm.

Declan's scalp throbbed from where the raven had grabbed a hunk of hair and pulled hard enough to rip it out by its roots. Malyn had a long scratch on one hand where he had fended off an attack.

"Got it." Kieron rose, holding the gem they had gotten from the vampire in the Deadlands high above his head. The sun glinted through the stone, sending crimson streaks of light all around them.

"Is this what you want?" Kieron shouted at the bird, staring it down as the raven gyred and dove straight for him. At the last second, the raven changed course, and its claws snatched the gem from Kieron's hand. Then it winged upward once more with a caw of victory.

The raven rose higher and then vanished into the tree canopy.

The companions looked at one another, nonplussed. "That's not exactly how I expected it to go," Kieron admitted.

"What did you bring me?"

The new voice startled them, and they spun to face the threat. A wizened, bent old man stood in front of the crypt door. Declan sensed his magic, and when he looked at the stranger, he had an odd double vision. He saw the old man, but he also saw a mummified corpse, with leathery skin drawn tight over bone, sharp teeth, and rheumy eyes. The old man's clothing hung in tatters from his hunched, bony form. He held out a claw-like hand for payment.

"It's Estan's other son," Declan warned the others. "The gatekeeper."

"No one passes, unless you've brought me what I require!" the gatekeeper demanded. He took a step toward them, and despite his guise as an old man, Declan saw the dark magic that animated the creature's true form.

"A gift or a soul. One or the other," the gatekeeper said. He eyed the group hungrily. "A half-elf would do nicely. Haven't had a soul like that in a long time."

"And you're not getting mine," Kane muttered, moving back and reaching for her bow.

"Easy," Malyn counseled.

She gave Malyn a withering glance but did not draw her weapon.

"And you, what a feast!" The gatekeeper turned his attention to Malyn, eyeing him like a tasty roast. "So many emotions. You would feed me for a long time."

Malyn's eyes narrowed, and Declan wondered what his friend's talent as a medium made of the undead guardian. "Go to the Pit," Malyn replied, his voice cold, gaze hard.

"Oh, I can never go there, that was the deal!" the gatekeeper said. "But if you didn't bring me what I need, I'll have your soul to feed me!"

In his guise as an old man, the gatekeeper looked deranged. But revealed in Declan's mage sight, the predator's eyes held a malicious glint as he sized up his potential victims.

"Such delicacies! A mage or a shifter? Hmm. Or a…human."

"We brought you a gift," Kieron replied, handing him the amulet and chain that had come with the Commissar's key from the Villa. He held it out to the old man, carefully keeping his fingers back from any contact.

The gatekeeper examined the amulet, holding it close to his eyes, giving it a sniff and a lick for good measure. It began to glow a dull, blood red and the gatekeeper smiled briefly before his visage returned to a scowl. He gave Kieron a disapproving look, perhaps unhappy to have his fun spoiled as he tucked the amulet into his rags.

"I'll take any goods you don't want to carry," the gatekeeper offered in a raspy voice. "Won't need them where you're going, and I wouldn't count on coming back." He turned and gestured to the gate.

Kieron shifted his pack on his shoulder and gave the gatekeeper a defiant look as he cautiously approached the gate, key in hand. "We'll be back," he said with assurance. "Now take your payment and let us pass."

The gatekeeper stepped aside, muttering under his breath. Declan kept a close eye on him, observing warily as Kieron turned the key and the lock gave an ominous *clunk*. Declan watched as Kieron tried to pull the key back out, but it held fast.

Malyn and Declan waited for Mitchell and Kane to go ahead. Malyn fixed the guardian with a glare, remaining turned toward him as Kieron pushed open the crypt doors on groaning hinges. Mitchell lit a lantern and held it aloft. Its light barely illuminated the first few steps inside.

"The underworld holds special terrors for one like you," the gatekeeper said as Malyn passed. "What's seen cannot be unseen."

Malyn didn't bother with a retort, but Declan saw a flash of fear in his friend's eyes as he followed the rest of them into the darkness. They left the door ajar, uncertain as to whether the door would open from this side. To get home, they needed to get to the next lychgate and use the first key. He doubted it would be as simple as the plan sounded.

Declan reminded himself that he wouldn't be making that trip. His passage through the gatekeeper's door was one-way, and he had left the world of the living behind him forever. The finality of his choice had settled over him on the long journey, and Declan felt at peace, knowing he would make it possible for the others to escape. Still, he could not avoid a bit of longing and a stab of sadness at the missed adventures yet to come. He had grown more than fond of his companions, and he hated the thought of leaving them.

Would part of him remain sentient, remembering? Perhaps. Malyn certainly spoke with ghosts who remembered their lives. Declan wasn't sure whether he would remain trapped on the Final Shore for his impudence in fighting Estan, or be permitted to cross over to... wherever the crossing took him. He hoped his friends would remember him kindly, and make the most of their victory and the bounty it brought them. Thinking of Kieron and the others happy on their farm, away from the hardship of Kortufan, made Declan feel satisfied.

"Remember the route," Malyn said, elbowing Declan with a look that the mage could not read. "We'll be coming back this way. All of us."

Declan wondered if his friend suspected something, but he did not correct him. Best if none of the others knew his plans, so they would not worry or try to stop him. They needed their attention focused on the quest, the splinter of the crown. *Damn, he would miss Malyn,* Declan thought before forcing himself to concentrate on their quest.

Declan called hand fire, holding the cold flicker aloft to help light the way. Kieron's lantern illuminated only a few feet in front of them, revealing a room hewn from the rock of the mountain, and a set of black stone stairs leading down. In the distance, Declan thought he heard the lap of waves.

Kieron and the others drew the knives they carried made of iron and steel, edged with silver. Estan might be god-bound to his post, but he was not a god himself. Undead or revenant, iron and silver would slow Estan, or perhaps dispel him long enough for them to retrieve their treasure.

Could Estan follow them back up the steps, or was his curse to remain on the Final Shore? Declan didn't know, and the book had not been specific. He intended to plant himself between Estan and the steps once they located the splinter, so that he could provide the distraction needed for the others to escape. With that in mind, Declan began gathering his power, grounding himself, and preparing to channel the most potent magic of his life, energy that would take everything he had and leave him hollow.

They staggered themselves on the steps so as not to present an easy target, with Kieron in the lead, hugging the left wall, then Mitchell a few steps up and to the right. Declan followed, on the left, then Kane, with Malyn bringing up the rear.

"The spirits know we're here," Malyn whispered. "They're curious. It's been a long time since any mortals came this way. Most are shades before they get this far."

"Are we being followed?" Kane asked quietly.

"I don't think so. If you mean the gatekeeper, then no. I think he got what he wanted…or at least had to settle for what we gave him," Malyn replied.

The upper cave where they entered had been musty and dry. As they descended, the rock walls grew moist, and the air held the scent of the sea. Odd, since to Declan's knowledge from their map they were nowhere near the ocean. His magic gave him no indication of other life in the darkness, and he heard nothing to suggest that they intruded upon insects or the small animals that often took refuge in caves. What Malyn made of it, with his ability to see spirits, Declan did not want to know.

The steep stairs led on for what felt like forever, darkness broken only by the light they brought with them. Eventually, a faint glow lit the bottom of the passageway, and the roar of waves echoed from the rock walls.

Kieron slipped from the shelter of the stairway, sliding along the wall to the right, while Mitchell edged out and went left. Declan moved up, biding his time. The map and the book said that the thief had driven his sword into the shore where he buried the splinter of the crown. A spot was marked on the drawing, but Declan wondered whether the sword would still be in place so long after its owner's death, or whether Estan had moved the splinter.

Curiosity won out over reluctance, and Declan edged closer to the opening to see. A huge cavern sprawled as far as the eye could see, lit by hundreds of torches in sconces that ringed the walls. A platform of rock extended from the base of the stairs, then a black sand beach stretched to the edge of a gray sea. Even from a distance, its waters looked cold and lifeless, and Declan could not repress a shiver. Beyond that sea lay whatever came next, when life was over, with Estan condemned to be the doorman to eternity.

Declan focused his magic and cast about the shimmer of power that would reveal the resonance of a relic as powerful as the splinter. Here below, on the doorstep to the underworld, magic felt strange, as if it belonged to the world of light and life. Or maybe it was just that everything about this chamber was magically-touched. A powerful presence was making its way closer, and Declan knew that once Estan arrived, it would be much more difficult to find the splinter. So he drew harder on his magic, paying special attention to the area of the dark sand where the map indicated the thief's treasure lay.

There. Declan felt the hum of an object with strong resonance, but its power felt fractured, as if it were a part of a missing whole. That convinced him that he had found the splinter, and he gestured to Kieron and Mitchell, who slipped along the rock wall before sprinting out in the open toward their prize. The two men fell to their knees and dug with their hands, sending the dark sand flying. There was no sword to mark their prize's location.

"He's coming." Malyn turned toward where the shoreline curved, ending in shadow in the far recesses of the cavern.

Kane moved forward, readying her bow with an arrow tipped with iron edged in silver. Malyn stood beside Declan, so that the three of them formed a barrier between the guardian of the Final Shore and Kieron and Mitchell, who were searching for the splinter.

"I've got this," Declan said.

Malyn fixed him with a glare. "Not alone, you don't."

Declan didn't argue. Instead, he anchored his magic, rooting himself in the bedrock and in the stone all around him, the bones of the world. He would draw from their strength, from the violence of their long-ago creation, and when that was not enough, he would empty himself, pulling from his life force, until there was nothing left.

Estan strode closer, a broad-shouldered man with an imperious gaze. He looked very much like his legend, a warrior nobleman-mage, trained for war and bred to privilege.

"Why have you come?" Estan demanded.

"We aren't here to trouble you," Malyn called back. Declan felt his friend's ghost magic rising, and was curious what effect it might have on a being like Estan, god-cursed to a half-life in the underworld.

"Yet you are here, in my domain. Alive. For now." Estan looked past them to where Mitchell and Kieron dug in the sand. "You have come for something that does not belong to you. Thieves! Treasure hunters! Despoilers of graves!"

"Hold on just a minute," Kane corrected. "We were sent here, by a demigoddess. You don't rightfully own the splinter—it was left here by the thief that stole it. We're returning it where it belongs."

"So you say," Estan countered. "The thief that buried it did not admit his guilt. I smote him and sent his soul for judgment."

"We don't need any smiting," Malyn replied in his most conciliatory voice. "Let us take what we came here for, and we'll leave quietly."

"Nobody leaves the Final Shores." Estan's booming voice echoed through the dark caverns. "However you came to be here, you belong to me, your lives are forfeit, and I will send your souls beyond the horizon."

"Not today." Kane let her arrow fly, and her aim was true. The iron and silver arrow hit Estan in the chest, a killing shot had he been mortal.

"Hurry!" Malyn shouted to Kieron and Mitchell. He extended one hand and closed his eyes, and the temperature fell as spirits flocked to his call.

How was that possible? Declan wondered. Estan's task lay in sending spirits across the Final Sea to rest or judgment. *Unless he's been as faithless in his punishment as he was in his vows to his liege lord?*

Ghosts massed around Estan at Malyn's call, a whirlwind of revenants whose shrieks and keens reverberated from the stone.

Declan seized the moment when Estan was at least temporarily affected by Kane's arrow and hedged in by angry spirits to channel a blast of magic and score a direct hit.

"We've got it!" Kieron said as he and Mitchell came bounding up.

Estan gave a furious roar, and the cloud of ghosts parted. He ripped the arrow from his chest, and the wound closed as if it had never been.

"Go!" Declan said. "I'll hold him. Take the splinter and go!"

"Like bloody hell we will," Kane retorted.

Declan spared enough concentration to give her a push toward the stairway. "Go!"

He turned his full attention to Estan. The ghosts returned to harry him, and no matter how often he swept them side, they came at him again and again, slowing his advance. Declan called on the spells he had not used since that last, disastrous duel, ones he had sworn he would never use again. They were potent, meant for desperate situations when nothing short of a suicide strike would suffice.

Everything else around him faded, and Declan poured all of his will and magic into the barrage. He didn't expect to destroy Estan, not if the treacherous warrior was, in fact, god-touched. But Declan didn't need to vanquish his foe. All he needed was to buy time for the others to escape with the splinter. Then Declan's work would be finished, and Estan could send him on across the dark sea.

Sight narrowed and hearing faded. Declan paid no heed to what was going on around him, as his focus tunneled to Estan, and he threw everything he had into his attack. Estan staggered back a step, then several more, as the blinding light of Declan's magic blasted him full in the torso. The screams of the dead echoed in the cave, and the storm of spirits lifted the black sand into the air in a violent swirl, nearly veiling Estan from sight.

Declan reached down deep, pulling on the energy of the cave, the bedrock, and his own soul for his final salvo. He hoped his friends had made it out, that he had won them enough time to make it up the steps and past the gatekeeper. Surely Estan would revive from the damage he suffered in this fight, but Declan would not. He prayed to Lady Leota that she would grant him the strength to speed their passage and get them home safely.

He felt an unexpected surge of power burning through him, lighting him on fire from within. Declan welcomed it, believing his prayer to be answered, and opened himself fully to its incandescent energy, a conduit to the magic that drove Estan back step by step until he fell into the dark sea, vanishing beneath its waves.

Abruptly the power was gone. Declan collapsed, utterly spent. He hoped it had been enough.

Rough hands lifted him and slung him over a muscular shoulder.

"No one stays behind," Mitchell rasped as he ran for the stairs, holding Declan in a rescue carry as he bounded up the stone steps. At least, that's what Declan thought he heard, as consciousness fled and he surrendered to nothingness.

KIERON

"RUN! I'VE GOT HIM," MITCHELL SHOUTED AS HE BOUNDED UP THE STAIRS. He passed the others who had waited with weapons drawn. They fell into place without prompting. This time, Kane took up the rear guard.

Kieron was the first to reach the crypt, panting and heaving for breath. He almost shouted for joy when he saw the door still stood ajar.

"Quick!" Kieron called after making sure no one was waiting for them on the other side. He held the door and felt the tension ease just a little as each of his friends bolted through the doorway. Once Mitchell was through, Kieron pulled the door closed and heard the lock click back into place.

He had the splinter of the crown, an unremarkable broken shard of old wood, inside a pouch on a strap around his neck, beneath his shirt. For all the trouble the splinter had caused, Kieron expected it to be set with jewels, painted with gold, or shine like the sun. After all they had gone through, it just didn't seem right that the splinter would be so ordinary. In fact, he had kept digging once they found it, thinking there must be something else, that the relic had to be more impressive. Whatever crown it was part of had to be the ugliest in history.

The others waited on the path, Kane and Malyn scanning the surrounding graveyard and road.

"Anything?" Kieron asked.

"No sign of the old man or the raven," Kane answered.

"You think it's safe to check him before we move on?" Kieron asked.

"I was going to anyway." Malyn approached and put his hand to the side of Declan's neck. "His heart is still strong. If you can carry him, Mitchell, let's get him to the lychgate before I try to do more."

"He's gangly and awkward but not all that heavy. I've got him." Mitchell gave Malyn a smile, the first Kieron had seen today.

They made their way down the path, still forced to move slowly through the briars and vines. At least this time the plants didn't seem to be intentionally holding them back, but progress was slow.

"The guardians are back," Kane announced.

"What?" Kieron turned from his place in the lead, sword drawn and ready.

"They're not following us, but the bird is perched on the gargoyle, and the old man watches from the steps." Kane shook her head as if she couldn't believe what she saw.

"Keep moving!" Kieron tried to cut more of the brush away that blocked their path but stayed alert in case the guardians or ghosts took exception to them relieving Estan of the wooden shard. It seemed even farther to the road than Kieron remembered and he couldn't help but feel relief when they reached the open space.

"Move as fast as you can, but don't let down your guard." Kieron turned to make sure everyone was with him. "The lychgate shouldn't be too much farther up the road. Stay wary." Kieron led on expecting an attack at any moment. Somehow he didn't think it would be quite so easy to leave with their prize.

"There's the lychgate. We're almost there," Kane called out.

"None too soon," Mitchell replied.

"There are ghosts following us," Malyn added as he glanced behind them.

"As long as they don't trip me up, or attack, I don't care," Mitchell snorted. He grunted as he adjusted Declan on his shoulder. "Okay, I admit it; he's heavier than I thought."

Kane and Malyn snickered. Kieron held it in but couldn't help the smile that spread across his face. He truly loved his friends, and while they didn't have the gold in hand yet, they were close enough that he could almost see the farmstead.

Kieron felt some of the tension release when they finally stepped into the protective wards of the lychgate. He helped Mitchell lay Declan out on the ground and stepped back as Malyn moved in.

"I told you he was going to sacrifice himself!" Malyn scowled as he ran his hands over Declan's still form. "Stubborn-arsed mage."

"Did he forget the part about we 'all' had to return to claim our reward?" Kane asked.

"I think he was too caught up in his own fears," Kieron sad sadly. "Like we'd ever leave him behind."

"Damn right," Malyn cursed. "We need him just as much as he needs us. From what I can tell, he's exhausted and he's probably going to have a splitting headache for a while, but I think I can help him." Malyn's hands glowed as he placed them on either side of Declan's temples.

"Did anyone else feel it? That surge at the end. It felt...different." Mitchell was pacing the length of the gate while Malyn attended to Declan.

"I did." Malyn looked up and caught Kieron's eye. "I think 'she' helped us."

"I was thinking the same," Mitchell said. He turned and saw Kane examining the post of the lychgate. "What?"

"I found the keyhole. Hopefully, that means the way home."

"Hey, when we build this place of ours, you think we could have our own rooms?" Mitchell asked.

"I don't see why not. It might take a while to build, but sure..."

"Hmph, maybe we could put in one of those special doors like they had at the monastery. You know, Mitchell-sized," Malyn teased.

"No, absolutely not. No telling what kind of foul thing might slip in," Kane objected.

They all laughed, even Mitchell. "I can manage a regular door, but thanks for thinking of me, Malyn."

Malyn sat back and gave Declan an appraising look. "I've done all I can. Now he needs rest." Malyn stood and dusted himself off.

"Let's go before anything else has a chance to attack," Kieron opened his pack and retrieved the first key, holding it out to Kane. "Would you do the honors?"

Kane smiled as she accepted the key and waited until everyone had queued up. She held her sword in the other hand. Malyn and Kieron also drew weapons and put Mitchell and Declan between them.

"Ready," Kieron said and held his breath as Kane turned the key.

TOM AT THE POXY DRAGON

"I DIDN'T HIT HIM WITH A BAR STOOL, AND I DIDN'T HIT HIM WITH A chair," Elsie argued, holding a bloodied rolling pin in one hand. "I just smacked him up the side of the head—lightly—with my roller because I didn't approve of his language."

Tom sighed and looked down at the unconscious man on the pub floor. "He's not even twitching. That was more than a 'smack.'"

Elsie leaned over for a closer look. "Pshaw. His skull's not crushed in none, now is it? Just a love tap, it was."

If that was a "love tap," Tom had an idea of what happened to Elsie's last husband. He wisely did not make that observation aloud.

Gunnar slid off his stool and ambled over, then knelt beside the man and felt for a pulse. Constance made a pass along the back wall, taking bets, and Benny the bard paused to gawk. Thaddeus gripped his shovel and edged closer, his expression hopeful and eyes alight.

"Still alive," Gunner announced.

Thaddeus slumped in disappointment and retreated to his place at the end of the bar, murmuring consolation to his shovel Bessie, which looked likely to remain unused that night. Constance paid out the winners, who joked and jeered, while the losers cursed and bemoaned their rotten luck. Benny struck up his song again, remembering where he had left off among the interminable verses.

"I'm just going to haul him over to the corner and put an empty tankard in his hand," Gunner said, hefting the unconscious man as if he weighed nothing, and dragging his limp form over to a chair by the wall. He propped the man up and arranged it so that he gripped a mug, making the unlucky fellow looked as if he had passed out from too much ale.

"There. When he comes around, he won't remember a thing," Gunnar said, stepping back to admire his handiwork.

"Except for the goose egg on the back of his noggin," Lucas pointed out helpfully as he bussed the next table. "But it's not where he's likely to see it. We can just say he banged his head when he passed out."

Tom ran a hand over his eyes and counted backward from ten. Tonight wasn't really any different than any other night at the Poxy Dragon. Benny caterwauled soulfully, accepting the coins the patrons threw at him and interpreting their contributions as requests to sing more, instead of a payoff to shut up.

Constance had only threatened to alter one difficult patron's manhood, meaning it was a slow evening.

Elsie had caught Lucas trying to sculpt bread dough into a gift of some sort for Constance and had taken after him with her spoon. The bruises would fade quickly.

Gunnar was already half a bottle into his quota for the evening, with hardly any evidence to prove it.

The patrons were the usual crew, here to see a fight or two and throw some darts or roll the dice, anything for a distraction. But Lady Leota looked twitchy, and Tom had learned to pay attention to such things. More than once she had glanced toward the boarded up window expectantly, and she had raised her head as if listening to a distant call, her expression unreadable. Leota's lips had moved silently, and her fingers wove an intricate pattern in the air before she slumped more than relaxed into her seat.

"You think they'll be back tonight?" Gunnar asked as he slid his glass across the bar for a refill.

"Maybe it won't be a total loss," Thaddeus said, stroking the handle of his shovel as if to reassure the implement it had a continued purpose.

Whatever Tom might have said was preempted, as the unused window glowed, revealing a swirl of stars and colors that stretched to infinity. Benny cut off his song mid-sentence and conversation stopped.

Elsie trooped in from the kitchen, and Lucas stood back, dirty dishes forgotten. Only Constance remained in motion, quickly taking bets from patrons before the portal disgorged its heroes and the opportunity to wager would be over.

The half-elf came through first, regaining her balance and coming up with a weapon in hand until she realized where she was. Next was the blond healer. The gateway dimmed.

Tom and Gunnar exchanged a glance, and Thaddeus leaned forward eagerly. *Where were the others?*

Then the portal flared again, and the shifter stumbled across the threshold, carrying the black-haired mage, followed by the human. The travelers paid no heed to anyone else in the pub, not even Lady Leota, as the shifter got his balance and gently set his injured companion on the floor, carefully propping him up against the wall.

"Should you check him again?" he asked the healer, who was already kneeling next to the mage.

The blond man knelt down and placed a hand over the mage's forehead and heart, and then stood, turning to Lady Leota.

"You did something, in the cave. I felt your energy. You must have, because otherwise, I don't think we would have made it."

Lady Leota gave a faint smile and inclined her head in acknowledgment. "When one of my champions has enough faith to call on me, I will heed the prayer."

The healer gave a low bow. "Thank you, my lady."

The human warrior stood and pulled out a pouch that hung around his neck, tucked into his tunic. He opened the pouch and dumped out a shard of wood into his hand, then approached Lady Leota warily, before carefully setting it on the table in front of her. His friends strained for a good look. "Here's the splinter of the crown. Not much to look at, for all the trouble it caused."

The demigoddess accepted the relic with an expression of reverence, taking it in her cupped hands and closing her eyes as if divining its essence. "Like you, it is so much more than it appears."

Leota opened her eyes and looked at the dirty, bloody misfit heroes who stood or knelt around the injured mage. "Your friend will be fine, though his willingness to sacrifice himself has been noted. You have all done well for me, my heroes." She regarded each of the party in turn. "Have you thought further about the boon you may ask of me? You have earned your reward."

The human leader exchanged a glance with his companions, and a silent conversation seemed to flow among them. The man turned back to Lady Leota and made a shallow bow. "My lady. We remain agreed on the purse of gold coins. We wish to buy a farm, far from the city, where we can live in peace, warm and with full bellies."

A smile played at the edges of the demigoddess's lips. "Very well then," she said and slid a pouch across the table. "You've earned your pay. And if I might make a suggestion," she added, "when you leave the city, look for a man named Piotr in the countryside near Cairn Rock, just south of here. I've heard he has land he's willing to part with. Tell him I sent you."

The human bowed again. "Thank you, my lady." The rest of his party except for the mage also bowed and echoed his thanks.

Lady Leota gave a discerning look to each of the heroes. "If you ever decide that your quiet life is not what you expected or have the urge for another adventure, come to see me."

The human gave a forced laugh. "Hardly likely, but thank you again, my lady."

Benny started in to a new ballad he had composed in the heroes' honor. Tom had heard him practicing, and knew that the song came with two endings and two tempos, depending on how the quest had turned out. Grumbling and hooting from the back of the bar made it clear that Constance was handling the bets, and that the majority had wagered against the heroes. Elsie muttered something and wandered back into the kitchen, with Lucas following, laden with dirty tankards.

"There's a room upstairs for you, on the house, if you'd rather not ride back tonight," Tom offered. One way or the other, Lady Leota's champions usually lingered at the Poxy Dragon when their quest was finished, either as temporary guests upstairs to recover, or permanent residents in the cemetery out back.

"Come on," the healer said, joining the shifter to help the mage get to his feet. "Let's let you sleep this off. We can get our things from the city in the morning, and go looking for that farm."

The group tromped up the stairs. Apparently they weren't interested in sticking around to hear the rest of Benny's song. Tom called after them, promising to send Lucas with food and drink. Tom glanced nervously over his shoulder, decided to give them bread, cheese, and sausage. Didn't feel quite right sending them Elsie's stew when they'd just done a good deed.

Constance brought the wager money to the bar, enough coins that she had filled her apron. "They were a popular bunch," she said. "I think that's a record for the house." Tom counted the coins and slipped her cut back across the sticky counter.

"Aye. If it weren't for bad luck, I'd have none at all," Thaddeus bemoaned, slumping next to Gunnar, with his shovel at his side.

Tom saw the look of defeat on Thaddeus's face and slid a glass of whiskey toward him. "Better luck next time," he said as the depressed undertaker accepted the drink and downed it in one slug.

"I hadn't really reckoned them for the farming type," Gunnar said, looking toward the stairs. "You think they'll make a go of it?"

Plenty of would-be champions came through the Poxy Dragon, most of them greedy braggarts who were interchangeable and easily forgettable. Tom realized he had actually been rooting for this misfit team, glad that they had survived and returned victorious.

"I think that if they can snatch a relic from the underworld and live to tell about it, their chances with chickens and cabbages are pretty good," Tom said. "That's a bet I'm even willing to place with Constance," he added, grinning.

"The next round is on the house," Tom shouted above Benny's awful singing. "All hail the heroes of the splintered crown!"

ACKNOWLEDGMENTS

A big thank you to my partner and oft-times co-author Gail Z. Martin, for her support, editing, and all the behind the scenes expertise she provides. Also thanks to our editor, Jean Rabe, cover artists Joachim Kornfeld ("Nathie" on DeviantArt) and Melissa McArthur, and our beta readers and launch team: Amy, Andrea, Anne, Bob, Cheryl, James, Jessy, Kyle, Laurie, Mindy, Renae, and Trevor. You helped to make this book the best it could be. Thank you also to the bloggers, reviewers, and signal boosters who help others hear about the book. I am deeply grateful to all of you, and this book wouldn't be possible without you. Thank you, most of all, to my readers, because you read, I write.

ABOUT THE AUTHOR

Larry N. Martin writes and co-authors science fiction, steampunk, and urban fantasy for Solaris books, Falstaff Books, Worldbuilders Press, and SOL Publishing. Prior to *The Splintered Crown*, the newest work was *Salvage Rat*, the first in a new space opera series. With Gail Z. Martin, Larry is co-author of the steampunk series *Iron and Blood: The Jake Desmet Adventures*, and a series of related short stories: *The Storm & Fury Adventures*, and *Spells, Salt, and Steel* set in the New Templar Knights universe. Short stories also appear in the anthologies *Cinched: Imagination Unbound*, *Afterpunk: Steam Powered Tales of the Afterlife*, *Clockwork Universe: Steampunk vs. Aliens*, and *Weird Wild West*. Also watch for two new series coming soon: Wasteland Marshals and The Joe Mack Shadow Council Files.

Where to find me, and how to stay in touch
On the web at LarryNMartin.com and on twitter @LNMartinAuthor.

Support Indie Authors
When you support independent authors, you help influence what kind of books you'll see and what types of stories will be available, because the authors themselves decide which books to write, not a big publishing conglomerate. Independent authors are local creators, supporting their families with the books they produce. Thank you for supporting independent authors and small press fiction!

ALSO BY LARRY N. MARTIN

Salvage Rat

The Splintered Crown: A Tankards and Heroes Novel

With Gail Z. Martin

Jake Desmet Adventures

Iron & Blood

Storm & Fury Collection

Spells, Salt, & Steel: New Templar Knights

Spells, Salt, & Steel: Season One

Spells, Salt, & Steel

Open Season

Deep Trouble

Close Encounters

Coming Soon

Cauldron: The Joe Mack Shadow Council Files

Wasteland Marshals

CPSIA information can be obtained
at www.ICGtesting.com
Printed in the USA
LVHW110022120922
728114LV00002B/241